S0-AAA-738

One Was Stubborn

SELECTED FICTION WORKS BY L. RON HUBBARD

FANTASY

The Case of the Friendly Corpse

Death's Deputy

Fear

The Ghoul

The Indigestible Triton

Slaves of Sleep & The Masters of Sleep

Typewriter in the Sky

The Ultimate Adventure

SCIENCE FICTION

Battlefield Earth

The Conquest of Space

The End Is Not Yet

Final Blackout

The Kilkenny Cats

The Kingslayer

The Mission Earth Dekalogy*

Ole Doc Methuselah

To the Stars

ADVENTURE

The Hell Job series

WESTERN

Buckskin Brigades

Empty Saddles

Guns of Mark Jardine

Hot Lead Payoff

A full list of L. Ron Hubbard's
novellas and short stories is provided at the back.

*Dekalogy—a group of ten volumes

L. RON HUBBARD

One Was Stubborn

GALAXY
PRESS

Published by
Galaxy Press, LLC
7051 Hollywood Boulevard, Suite 200
Hollywood, CA 90028

© 2013 L. Ron Hubbard Library. All Rights Reserved.

Any unauthorized copying, translation, duplication, importation or distribution,
in whole or in part, by any means, including electronic copying, storage or
transmission, is a violation of applicable laws.

Mission Earth is a trademark owned by L. Ron Hubbard Library and
is used with permission. *Battlefield Earth* is a trademark owned
by Author Services, Inc. and is used with permission.

Horsemen illustration from *Western Story Magazine* is © and ™ Condé Nast
Publications and is used with their permission. Cover art; "One Was Stubborn" and
"A Can of Vacuum" story illustrations; Fantasy, Far-Flung Adventure and Science
Fiction illustrations and Glossary illustrations: *Unknown* and *Astounding Science
Fiction* copyright © by Street & Smith Publications, Inc. Reprinted with permission
of Penny Publications, LLC. "240,000 Miles Straight Up" story illustrations
and Story Preview cover art: © 1948 Standard Magazines, Inc.
Reprinted with permission of Hachette Filipacchi Media.

Printed in the United States of America.

ISBN-10 1-59212-370-8
ISBN-13 978-1-59212-370-4

Library of Congress Control Number: 2007927676

Contents

Stories from Pulp Fiction's Golden Age

A ND it *was* a golden age.

The 1930s and 1940s were a vibrant, seminal time for a gigantic audience of eager readers, probably the largest per capita audience of readers in American history. The magazine racks were chock-full of publications with ragged trims, garish cover art, cheap brown pulp paper, low cover prices—and the most excitement you could hold in your hands.

"Pulp" magazines, named for their rough-cut, pulpwood paper, were a vehicle for more amazing tales than Scheherazade could have told in a million and one nights. Set apart from higher-class "slick" magazines, printed on fancy glossy paper with quality artwork and superior production values, the pulps were for the "rest of us," adventure story after adventure story for people who liked to *read.* Pulp fiction authors were no-holds-barred entertainers—real storytellers. They were more interested in a thrilling plot twist, a horrific villain or a white-knuckle adventure than they were in lavish prose or convoluted metaphors.

The sheer volume of tales released during this wondrous golden age remains unmatched in any other period of literary history—hundreds of thousands of published stories in over nine hundred different magazines. Some titles lasted only an issue or two; many magazines succumbed to paper shortages during World War II, while others endured for decades yet. Pulp fiction remains as a treasure trove of stories you can read, stories you can love, stories you can remember. The stories were driven by plot and character, with grand heroes, terrible villains, beautiful damsels (often in distress), diabolical plots, amazing places, breathless romances. The readers wanted to be taken beyond the mundane, to live adventures far removed from their ordinary lives—and the pulps rarely failed to deliver.

In that regard, pulp fiction stands in the tradition of all memorable literature. For as history has shown, good stories are much more than fancy prose. William Shakespeare, Charles Dickens, Jules Verne, Alexandre Dumas—many of the greatest literary figures wrote their fiction for the readers, not simply literary colleagues and academic admirers. And writers for pulp magazines were no exception. These publications reached an audience that dwarfed the circulations of today's short story magazines. Issues of the pulps were scooped up and read by over thirty million avid readers each month.

Because pulp fiction writers were often paid no more than a cent a word, they had to become prolific or starve. They also had to write aggressively. As Richard Kyle, publisher and editor of *Argosy,* the first and most long-lived of the pulps, so pointedly explained: "The pulp magazine writers, the best of them, worked for markets that did not write for critics or attempt to satisfy timid advertisers. Not having to answer to anyone other than their readers, they wrote about human beings on the edges of the unknown, in those new lands the future would explore. They wrote for what we would become, not for what we had already been."

Some of the more lasting names that graced the pulps include H. P. Lovecraft, Edgar Rice Burroughs, Robert E. Howard, Max Brand, Louis L'Amour, Elmore Leonard, Dashiell Hammett, Raymond Chandler, Erle Stanley Gardner, John D. MacDonald, Ray Bradbury, Isaac Asimov, Robert Heinlein—and, of course, L. Ron Hubbard.

In a word, he was among the most prolific and popular writers of the era. He was also the most enduring—hence this series—and certainly among the most legendary. It all began only months after he first tried his hand at fiction, with L. Ron Hubbard tales appearing in *Thrilling Adventures, Argosy, Five-Novels Monthly, Detective Fiction Weekly, Top-Notch, Texas Ranger, War Birds, Western Stories,* even *Romantic Range.* He could write on any subject, in any genre, from jungle explorers to deep-sea divers, from G-men and gangsters, cowboys and flying aces to mountain climbers, hard-boiled detectives and spies. But he really began to shine when he turned his talent to science fiction and fantasy of which he authored nearly fifty novels or novelettes to forever change the shape of those genres.

Following in the tradition of such famed authors as Herman Melville, Mark Twain, Jack London and Ernest Hemingway, Ron Hubbard actually lived adventures that his own characters would have admired—as an ethnologist among primitive tribes, as prospector and engineer in hostile climes, as a captain of vessels on four oceans. He even wrote a series of articles for *Argosy,* called "Hell Job," in which he lived and told of the most dangerous professions a man could put his hand to.

Finally, and just for good measure, he was also an accomplished photographer, artist, filmmaker, musician and educator. But he was first and foremost a *writer,* and that's the L. Ron Hubbard we come to know through the pages of this volume.

This library of Stories from the Golden Age presents the best of L. Ron Hubbard's fiction from the heyday of storytelling, the Golden Age of the pulp magazines. In these eighty volumes, readers are treated to a full banquet of 153 stories, a kaleidoscope of tales representing every imaginable genre: science fiction, fantasy, western, mystery, thriller, horror, even romance—action of all kinds and in all places.

Because the pulps themselves were printed on such inexpensive paper with high acid content, issues were not meant to endure. As the years go by, the original issues of every pulp from *Argosy* through *Zeppelin Stories* continue crumbling into brittle, brown dust. This library preserves the L. Ron Hubbard tales from that era, presented with a distinctive look that brings back the nostalgic flavor of those times.

L. Ron Hubbard's Stories from the Golden Age has something for every taste, every reader. These tales will return you to a time when fiction was good clean entertainment and the most fun a kid could have on a rainy afternoon or the best thing an adult could enjoy after a long day at work.

Pick up a volume, and remember what reading is supposed to be all about. Remember curling up with a *great story.*

—Kevin J. Anderson

KEVIN J. ANDERSON *is the author of more than ninety critically acclaimed works of speculative fiction, including The Saga of Seven Suns, the continuation of the Dune Chronicles with Brian Herbert, and his* New York Times *bestselling novelization of L. Ron Hubbard's* Ai! Pedrito!

One Was Stubborn

Author's Note

*T*his present manuscript is a paraphrase of one which is very
   strange indeed. I have included in it all its essentials and have
removed from it only that which was rambling and incoherent.
The original came to me in the hands of a peculiar old fellow
who was admitted for treatment to Balm Springs. He had a very
stubborn quality about him which made him nearly impossible
to treat, and this intractability earned for him the pseudonym of
Old Shellback among the interns and psychiatrists.

Oddly, he came with no past history and refused to give any. No
one could learn, for some time, where he had been born or whether
he had any people alive. And then, one day, with a rock-jawed
glare at my insistence, he said:

"My mother and father have yet to be born. If I have any
ancestors living in this country now I am positive I won't see them.
The place I was born will not be built for another three hundred
years and, when I was born in it, it was already two hundred
and fifty years old. It is gone because it has yet to exist. It will be
gone thereafter because it will cease to exist.

"I am a negative five hundred and ninety years old. Tomorrow,
my birthday, I shall be a negative five hundred and eighty-nine.
I have less than thirty years of life expectancy remaining to me
and so I shall not live to be more than a negative five hundred
and sixty years.

3

"What has happened to me has happened because of what happened to the Universe. But mainly because there is but one god and his name will be George Smiley.

"You haven't tried to make me do anything. Therefore I shall give you the manuscript which explains this. I wrote it when I was marooned a little while, about eighty years from now, in Paris just after the United States began to rebuild it."

And so he brought me the manuscript. It had evidently been written under stress, for the first half-dozen pages are illegible as compared to the graceful script of the remainder.

Old Shellback grew restless after he had been with us six or seven months, for he seemed to sense danger in all clocks. In fact a man had only to take out a watch and Old Shellback would dive for his cubicle and refuse to come forth the rest of the day. Then he began to mutter, over and over, "Not far enough back. Not far enough back. Not far enough back." Nothing could be found as the cause of this, but Old Shellback seemed to think the menace quite valid. And then one day he came rushing into my office—it was a New Year's Day—and demanded his original manuscript which, of course, I gave him. I had no thought of what he might do and what he did was quite startling.

Old Shellback was seen to lock himself into his room. There was no egress therefrom.

An hour later, when he would not respond, we forced the door. On the bed was a scrawled note:

"My apologies to Dr. LaFayette. But this is not far enough back, you see. Not far enough back!"

Old Shellback was gone!

4

One Was Stubborn

I thought it was my vision.

For some time my wife had been nagging me about glasses, telling me that I ought to get those Brilloscopes that were always being advertised on the three-dimensional color television. But somehow the more I heard "See like a cat and feel like a million with Brilloscopes, the Invisible Optic Aids," the less inclined I was to get a pair.

And so when I beheld a pair of legs walking toward me all by themselves, I, of course, concluded that it was my vision. In fact, for some days things had been getting slightly misty and the mist was deepening. But to see a pair of legs with pants neatly pressed and shoes precisely tied walk up to you and by you and around the corners—well, even I could see that I must give in.

I stepped onto the express conveyer belt and went whizzing off toward the Medical Center, and as I sped along I again received a shock. The great glistening domes of Science Center, usually so plainly seen from all levels of the city save the third trucking tier under the glass subways, were missing one of their number. I supposed, of course, that the Transstellar Express might have swished too close to it on the night before, but I was wrong. For when I diverted my eyes for

5

a moment to avoid being struck by a fat woman's antigravity cane and then looked through the invisible super-levels at the place where the dome had been, the dome was back in place! I certainly did need glasses!

I was so groggy when I stepped off the conveyer belt and grabbed the scoop which lifted up to the medical department level that I didn't even see a crazy college student swing off Level 20 in his antique Airable Swishabout—one of those things with signs over the dents saying, "Eve, Here's Your Atom," and "Ten Tubes All Disintegrating," and "Hey, Babe, didn't we meet on Mars?" You know the menace. Well, one of those blasted straight at me and I didn't even have time to duck—and I probably couldn't have anyway, thanks to my rheumatism.

And if I had been startled before, I was prostrate now. That Swishabout rattled to the right and left and above and below and was gone. I'd passed all the way through it!

I was almost scared to let go of the bucket and step out on the Eye Level for fear the invisible walk was not only invisible but also not there!

Somehow I hauled myself up to the sorting psycher while the beam calculators sized me up and then, when the flasher had blinked "Dr. Flerry" as its decision for me, I managed to sink down on the sofa which whisked me into his office.

The nurse smiled pleasantly and said, "Nervous disability is quite easy to correct and Dr. Flerry is expert. Please be calm."

"I haven't got any nervous disability," I said. "I came up here to get tested for some glasses."

She looked at one of those confounded charts that the

sorting psycher forwards ahead of the patient, and when I saw her finger come down to "Stubborn" I knew she'd nod. She did. A thoroughly unmanageable young woman.

"You haven't been brought to an eye doctor," she said. "Dr. Flerry treats nervous disability only, as you must know."

"I came for an eye test," I said, "and I'm going to get an eye test. I don't give a flimdoodle what that blathery card says; it's *eyes*. Do you think a machine knows more about me than I do?"

"Sometimes a machine does. Now please don't get upset."

"I'm not upset. I guess I know when I need glasses and when I don't need glasses. And if I want to be tested for glasses, I pretty well guess I'll be tested for glasses!"

"You," she said, "are obviously a stubborn sort of fellow."

"I guess," I said, "that I am the most stubborn fellow in this city if not in this whole country."

"Don't tell me," she said.

Well, I don't know why, but I felt a little better after that. And shortly, Dr. Flerry buzzered me into his inner office. He was one of these disgusting young fellows who think they know so much about the human body that they themselves can't be human.

"Now be calm," he said, "and tell me just what the trouble is." He seemed to be in a sort of ecstatic state and he didn't seem to take me seriously enough.

"I won't be calm," I said, "and I don't have to tell you what the trouble is. You've got a psycher chart there that will tell you all about me even down to my last wart."

"Yes," he said, "you do have a wart. I shall have Dr. Dremster remove it before you go."

"You won't touch any wart of mine," I said. "I came in here to get a pair of glasses, and by the Eternal, I'll get them if I have to sit here all night."

I guess I had him there, for he sat and stared at me for some little time before he replied.

Finally he said, "Now just what is making you nervous?"

"I am *not* nervous!" I shouted. "I want glasses!"

"Ah," he said. And then he sat back and pushed his head against a pad so the mechanical chair arm would put a lighted cigarette in his mouth. "My dear fellow, tell me just why you need a pair of glasses."

"Because I need them, that's why!"

"Reading glasses?"

"Reading glasses!" I said. "I never read any of the bilge the papers are ordered to publish."

"Then you watch the televisor quite a bit?"

"I wouldn't turn one of those things on for a million dollars. What do you ever hear but advertising and smoky bands, and what do you see but girls with legs? Bah!" I guess I was telling him now.

"Ah," he said and thumped back with an elbow so that his chair's arm would pour him a glass of water. "But you don't need glasses to talk to people."

"I never talk to people. I never talk to anybody except my wife and I don't talk to her and she doesn't listen to me any more than I listen to her. She never says three words a week to me anyway." Which is the way things should be, of course.

"What, may I ask, is your business?"

"You've got a nerve to ask, but for your information I haven't got any business. I retired off my farm about four years ago and I haven't spent a happy hour since."

"Ah," he said.

"Don't sit there saying 'Ah' like an idiot," I said. "Get busy and fit me with a pair of glasses."

"You haven't said why you needed them. You can have them of course, but to give them to you I'll have to know just what sort of glasses you mean. What convinced you that you should have them?"

I could see that I had scared Dr. Flerry into being polite to me, so I told him that I had seen a pair of legs without a torso and had first missed and then seen one of the Medical Center domes and how that crazy college student had run right through me.

Well, if Dr. Flerry hadn't stopped laughing when he did I guess we would have mixed it up right then.

"What's so funny?" I demanded.

"Why, my dear fellow," said Dr. Flerry, "you don't need any glasses. If you ever paid any attention to the newspapers or the televisors or talked to anyone, you'd understand what is happening."

"And what," said I, "is happening?"

"Why, my dear fellow, is it possible that you haven't heard of the Messiah?"

"Him," I said. "What about *him*?"

"Would you care to come around to our meeting tonight? You might be edified."

9

"I don't like meetings. I don't believe in meetings."

"But my dear fellow, the Messiah will—"

"I don't believe in messiahs."

"Well, however that may be, I wonder at you. You are probably the only man in the world today who is not a follower. Let me explain to you what this is all about so that—"

"I don't want to know anything about it and I wouldn't believe it if I did."

"Nevertheless, let me tell you something of this. The Messiah from Arcturus Arcton is teaching the nonexistence of matter. You see, by that he means that all matter is an idea. And it is high time that the world was relieved from the crushing load of materialism which has almost quenched the soul of man. Those are his words. And it's true. Man is being pushed all around by machines and the age of machines has been over for a century, but the machines just keep running, and man, because he is so lazy, keeps using them. Now it may surprise you that a man such as myself, dependent upon the ills of the body as I am, should advocate the loss of the body. But I get no real interest out of my trade, for everything about the body is known except, of course, the soul and the Messiah has a good line on that. Further, in common with the rest of humanity, I am bored. I am so bored that I welcome any diversion. And I know that all this material world and this body I drag around are useless sources of annoyance.

"Now the Messiah is teaching us the folly of belief. So long as we believe in this world, this Universe, in machines and ills and mankind, then mankind shall survive and the world, the Universe and machines shall survive. But as soon as we lose all belief in these things, then we shall be freed. We shall be freed, my friend, from the agony caused by machines and other men. And, being slaves to cogwheels, the only answer is to abolish the very matter from which those same cogwheels and these bodies are made. Well! Matter does not really exist, you know. It is only a figment of our imaginations. We believe in matter and so there is matter. That, my dear fellow, is the glorious message you have missed by not listening or reading."

"You mean," I said, "that everybody belongs to this?"

"Certainly. Hasn't the whole world been miserable ever since all further advance was unattainable? And isn't this the one answer to our misery?"

"But . . . but where will everyone go?" I said.

"Why, we return to our proper position as a compound idea. And there we shall have nothing that is miserable or worrying—"

"But you won't even exist!"

"Certainly not," he said with a tired smile. And he nudged with his elbow and tilted his head back while his chair's arm poured another glass of water down his throat. Languidly then he nodded to me.

"You don't need glasses, my dear fellow. You are only witnessing the fruits of our combined disbelief. Several people happened to disbelieve that dome and then the college student probably didn't believe in his Swishabout, and you, about to be killed by it, refused to believe in it either. So come around to our meeting tonight and hear all about it. It is really quite fascinating." He yawned in boredom and pushed a pedal which shot my sofa car out to the Eye Level again.

11

I stepped on a down bucket. Wouldn't it be awful, I thought, if this bucket didn't exist? But it evidently still did and nothing happened until I was being speeded home on the conveyers.

The Trans-System 5:15 Local roared away from its field to the north and when it had attained the zenith it suddenly vanished. There wasn't so much as a puff of smoke left in the sky. And about ten seconds later it appeared again fifty or sixty miles up, visible because of its exhaust flames in the dusk.

When I got home I went to bed behind a locked door. The bed, at least, showed no sign of vanishing. And if things were going to persist in refusing to exist, I vowed I wouldn't leave that room until my condensochow and my stock of Old Space Ranger gave out.

I went out three times in three weeks and twice I came back so badly unnerved that again I barricaded myself. For the things which were happening clearly showed that the world had gone completely mad and maybe not only the world but the Universe as well. I recalled a fragment of talk I had heard concerning the disease machine madness, and I was now convinced that the disease had invaded everyone. And that it was even invading me.

My wife hadn't spoken to me for so long that one day when she stuck her head in the door and announced that a gentleman was here to see me, I noticed for the first time that all was not well with her. She had a sort of ecstatic fixity about her face that could not even be broken by animosity toward me.

The gentleman came in. He had a robe of blue flashtex wrapped around him so that he was mostly hypnotic eyes. He said, "My name is George Smiley. I am called the Messiah!"

I must admit that I was never so close to being frightened in my life. He brought down his arm a little and exposed his face and if I have ever in my life seen anything sardonic it was the grin he wore. He was not handsome nor tall, but there was some kind of presence to him which would have singled him out from a million made up exactly like him.

"What do you want with me?" I said.

"I merely wish to speak with you."

"Then go ahead," I said.

"A Dr. Flerry, Number 483,936,3297,024AG, has reported to me that you may be the one responsible for the way things are progressing. We have done away with the disbelief of some thousands like you and you are the last one. I understand that you have neither heard nor read of the Great Eclipse."

I couldn't look him in the eyes and so I watched the way his flashtex cape rippled. "All I know is what Dr. Flerry told me."

"And still you were not interested enough to attempt to believe with the rest?"

"Why should I be interested?" I said.

"Because this vitally concerns your happiness. Have you no wish to defeat the mechanism and organization which has enslaved mankind? Have you no desire to liberate yourself from the toils of a miserable existence?"

"I can do that with a splashgun," I said. "I don't have to believe in you to do it."

"Ah! And there you are wrong. If you kill yourself, you will not share. Is there no way to convince you that our precepts are the only precepts?"

"I can grow cabbage," I said. "And I can milk cows. And I have stayed healthy so far by not listening to anybody on the subject of anything. You are wasting your time with me."

"You mean you refuse?"

"I guess that's what I mean."

"You are a very stubborn man."

"I believe what I want to believe. I believe this is a world. And anybody that tries to tell me that this glass and bottle are not real is going to get an awful argument from me."

"Then," said George Smiley, the Messiah, "my hand is forced. I sent no minions. I came myself. You are the last man. I and the rest of the Universe shall cease to believe in your soul and you shall cease to exist. Good day."

"Good day," I said.

He looked back once from the door. I was trying to pour myself a drink but the bottle neck chattered against the glass and the Old Space Ranger spilled. I felt his eyes.

And then there weren't a bottle and a glass in my hands! I held nothing!

"Good day," he said again in a cheerful voice. He was gone.

During the remainder of that day I did nothing more than sit and look at the patterns in the fluffoplex floor. I was half angry, half scared, and I was trying my best to understand just what George Smiley, the Messiah, was doing. I have been told that I have a suspicious nature. However that may be, I suspected George Smiley. Every person I had seen for weeks, now that I came to think about it, had had that same strange fixity of expression which my wife had borne; just as though everyone had become a saint.

It was much against my principles to surrender to the extent of examining the problem but, at last, when night— as I thought—had come, I went into the next room and fumbled around until I found what papers my wife had accumulated during the past month or two. I sat and read, then, for nearly two hours.

But at the end of that time I was not even close to a solution. All I discovered was that George Smiley had come from Arcton with a message. Of course, I knew that everyone in the Universe was bored and would welcome any kind of diversion and that such a time, according to my Tribbon's *Rise and Fall of the American Empire,* provided unscrupulous men with a host of willing dupes for religious experimentation. That many of these had been maniacs was a fact which Tribbon, the great unbeliever, italicized. But, so far in history, no one man had managed to swing a nation, much less the Universe, around to his method of thinking. But it had been so long since any man had had to develop an original idea that almost any idea would have been acceptable. I suppose that it was the perfection of communication which made it possible for George Smiley to reach everyone everywhere. And the freedom which the Machine Magistration gave all religious exponents accounted for George Smiley's not being stopped.

And, worse luck, it seemed that I was the only man left that didn't want to slip off into the limbo.

It had already been proved that mass concentration could do away with material objects but that fact was so old that, until now, it had lain dormant except in the pranks of schoolboys who, learning about it for the first time, vanished desks out from in front of their professors.

George Smiley, according to these reports, was a virile fellow who had lived alone for years and years as a prospector on Arcton. But the fact that his parents were not known made me believe that perhaps both his father and his mother had finished this life as members of the famous Arcton Prison to which so many universal criminals were shipped. Did this George Smiley have a grudge against the whole Universe?

That sardonic smile of his and those terrifying eyes—

Well! It wasn't going to do me any good to sit and moon over the papers. Besides I felt I had better put them back before my wife found that I was reading them. Such surrender was unthinkable. Accordingly I walked out into the living room—

And fell!

There must be ground under me!

I lit!

And then I sat there, staring all about me in helpless bewilderment.

There wasn't any living room anymore. Maybe . . . maybe my own room—

No, there was no sign of that either.

The papers! The papers I had been holding in my hand—

For a second one sheet rustled and then it, too, faded away.

There was something solid under me but that was all the solidity anywhere.

Accordingly I walked out into the living room—
And fell!

The city, perhaps the world, perhaps everything, was a flood of gray and curling mist! I felt of myself and was relieved to know that I was still myself anyway. For an instant I had wondered and, wondering, had felt myself thin and pale. But I was again solid and that upon which I was seated was still ground and so I took slight heart.

What, I wondered, had happened to my wife? And what had happened to the house? And the city? Certainly there must be something left of the city. And I began to feel that if I couldn't find something of it I should certainly go mad.

No more condensochow. No more Old Space Ranger. Oh, my goodness, yes, I had to find the city.

I stood up and groped before me, my hands nearly invisible in the murk. Step by step I found ground and, once, I thought I saw the corner of a building but, when I approached it closely, it, too, was gone.

For what seemed an hour I floundered about without being able to locate a street. I was getting angry, probably because I was getting scared. I consulted my watch and found out that it was half past ten. For what seemed a long while I kept on working along, expecting any moment to find a wall or a conveyer belt or a parked autoairbile but each next moment being disappointed. Finally I again looked at my watch; it was still half past ten. I thought that I must have missed the hands the first time in the absence of light but there was no missing them now, for the dial glowed softly and the mist itself seemed to have some quality of illumination. And then, having groped for what seemed yet a third half-hour, I looked once more at my watch. It was still half past ten!

Had something happened to Time?

Was I adrift in something which wasn't Space?

There were no quizclickers gaping for their pennies and their questions on each lamppost anymore, and so I had to try and answer it myself.

Yes, there was Space. I could feel myself and I knew I moved and so there must be Space. If it took me time to move— Perhaps, I thought, I had better locate someone else before I went completely mad.

For all this murk was seeping into my heart; like drifting smoke it curled and wound and spired, leaving black alleys stretching endlessly out and then rolling in upon the openings and swallowing them, leaving towers which stretched an infinity up and down and then devouring the towers. The very solidity on which I trod was hidden. There was no direction to anything and I felt that I might well be upside down or horizontal for all I knew. And I might not be walking on anything at all—

And at that thought I began to fall. And falling, I feared earth. And fearing earth, I landed. I was ill. The thought that I must keep earth in mind or fall again was enough to make me do just that. And when again I was upon solidity I understood that I might drop an infinity, step by step, and never arrive at anything.

With great suddenness it came to me that so long as I believed in myself, I was. So long as I believed, there was

Space. I was adrift in a murky ocean of mist, drowned in an immensity of nothingness, marooned in nonexistence.

I must find somebody.

I could not tolerate being alone.

And so I stumbled forward, groping hopefully. I was not used to walking any more than anyone else had been used to it. And I began to tire. I had fallen far, I knew and, I supposed, I would have to rise again to the same altitude of the city's site before I could discover anything.

But I was wrong. I had begun to wish violently for a bucket to bear me upward and then, banging my shins, I ran into the bucket. I had been wandering so long and so far without any contacts that I gripped that bucket as one grips a lost friend found again. Joyously I put my feet upon it. Gratefully I sank into its fluffoplex arms. And upward I went.

I was almost certain now that I had sunk no lower than the fifth level subsurface, for there the buckets began, and so I waited patiently for the conveyance to gently alight me upon a higher level. But I just kept on going up. Ordinarily it used to take a bucket not more than a minute to lift anyone twenty levels. But I realized that I had been sitting there at least five minutes, ascending swiftly through impenetrable mist.

In sudden panic I wondered where I was going. No bucket I had ever seen could have gone as high as this. Why . . . why, I must be on a level with the Court Domes. Or— God help me, I must be about to crash through the Weather Roof!

Suddenly I beheld a glass pane above. The bucket hit it squarely and rebounded. Madly I gripped at the chair arms.

What if this bucket should vanish? What if the bucket, too, should cease to be? And it did.

I fell through the giddy mists. Only an aircab could have saved me. And then I wasn't falling. I was sitting in an aircab.

For several seconds I just sat there, clinging thankfully to the seat, not thinking at all about where I might be going. The driver must have seen me falling and zipped under me and was waiting now for me to recover my breath before he asked my destination. I leaned past the meter.

"Thank you," I said. "If you'll take me to the Food Central, I'll be very grateful."

A face . . . a face and nothing more glowed briefly above the bar control and a voice snarled, "You can't do this to me. Who the hell do you think you are?" And the face was gone and the aircab went purring along, utterly driverless.

I was shaken, for it took me some time to understand just what was happening to me. I felt that if I went on like this much longer without the solace of a drink, I should perish. Oh, for a little snort of Old Space Ranger!

I drank it off and instantly felt better.

And then I felt worse.

I hadn't been carrying a glass of Old Space Ranger around with me all this time! And there wasn't anyone about who could have placed it in my hand!

And yet I had just had a drink!

And instead of being in that aircab I was sitting on nothing!

What had happened to the aircab? Certainly I still must be in it!

And there I was, purring along in the aircab again.

"Driver," I said, "I don't understand—"

"Don't try it on me!" snarled a face beside the meter. It vanished, all but the eyes, and these were so malevolent that I looked away.

The aircab vanished, too.

I sat very still on whatever this solidity was and tried to get myself straightened out. I had spoken to that driver twice and each time he had almost appeared. And I felt that the next time I tried to bring him out he would certainly deal roughly with me after the way of hackies. Each time I had imagined things it seemed that those things had come to pass.

Was I, then, a figment of my own imagination?

Shiver the thought!

Could I bring anything I wanted into being with my own thought? In his *Rise and Fall of the American Empire,* Tribbon hinted at the future possibility that the world and even the Universe might be destroyed by combined thought, the world and the Universe evidently being nothing but an idea. Had humanity committed mass suicide or mass combination to the exclusion of matter? And was I, then, the only one left whose belief in his own individuality was so great that that individuality still existed? And being the only individual mind still possessed by a man, could I create at will?

Or was I doomed for ever and ever to drift aimlessly through this clammy mist, timeless and alone?

I could not bear the thought. Tribbon had stated that man's one redeeming feature was his own ability to create, and that he, therefore, assigned creativeness to God. And Tribbon had said that when man no longer created, then man would no longer be. I had been the last manual farmer. Was I then the last man with ability to create?

Certainly if anything could be saved or if anything could exist, then it must be created by myself.

That was it!

I must create!

I glowed with the idea. I walked around on my created solidity and laughed aloud. Always before I had had to callous my hands and besweat my brow, but now I only had to think. And what things wouldn't I create! I came as close to dancing as I ever did in all my life.

The mist!

I would create sunlight!

With all my wit I concentrated, and then! Then a shaft of light came from somewhere and played its beam upon me and warmed my rheumatic bones.

Sunlight!

By my own imagination I could bring to being light and warmth and cheer! I sang out, so great was my joy.

Now let me create a meadow. A meadow which I would surround with trees and cross with a brook. I closed my eyes and concentrated and, when I opened them again, there was the meadow!

I started to caper out into the tall grass and then, midpace, stopped dead still. What had happened to the sunlight? The mist so befogged this meadow that it could scarcely be seen. Sunlight!

Sunlight!

And there it came again, that pleasant, golden beam.

But as soon as the sunlight came, the meadow vanished!

How uncertain all this was! Was it possible that I could create but not enduringly? That I could create and maintain only one object at a time? Did these things depend wholly upon my ability to concentrate upon them?

And even while I pondered the question, the sunlight faded before the mist and I was again surrounded by the clammy grayness. But for all my disappointment, I had established one thing: that I could bring things into being even if I could not maintain them.

Certainly there must be some solution to this sort of thing. If I gave it enough thought, perhaps I could manage a way to trap sunlight and meadows into reality.

I sat down upon my solidity and pursed my lips and stroked my chin. Try as I might I could not remember if Tribbon had had anything to say upon the subject of concentration.

I thumbed hopefully through the index, but the only reference close to it was "Concentration Camps: New York, San Francisco, Washington." I stared into the mist a while and when I looked back at the book, it was gone. Oh, well, I thought, I would rather have some Old Space Ranger anyway.

I drank it off.

And it made me hungry.

So I ate the steak.

Feeling better, I again got restless. I could not sit around on an imagined solidity for all eternity. I could call down the sunlight at will, but I couldn't keep it there, and so I gave over. And then it occurred to me that the reason I thought I was standing upon something was because I had always stood upon something and was so used to the idea that I could not shake it.

And the instant it became an "idea" only, I fell. And I became scared. And I landed.

If I could only talk this over with someone, I sighed. But I was careful not to think I saw anyone, for people did not seem to like being hauled back from wherever they had gone. Certainly somewhere in all this there must be at least one other man. To think that I was the only one was conceit of the most outrageous kind. Somewhere there was somebody. And if he and I could just get together then he might know enough and I might know enough to put some semblance of a world together and keep it together.

Again I wandered—and floundered—and fell when I thought about my solidity—and landed—and pawed through this endless mist.

Once or twice I thought I saw people. But I could not be sure, for I was careful not to think they *were* people. And when I had spent a timeless space in stumbling about I forgot my caution and, seeing a misty thing which looked like a man, thought he *was* a man.

Very briefly he assumed a shape. It was nebulous and distorted as though I looked at him through a drinking glass just emptied of milk.

"Stop it!" he cried in a thin voice. "By what right have you dragged me back? Vanish and be saved!"

And he vanished.

From somewhere came caroling voices and an ineffably sweet harmony which I could not associate with any instruments I had ever heard. For an instant there came over me an exquisite longing to forget myself and my misery and join that chorus. But then I remembered Flerry and George Smiley and, doggedly, I went on with my search. Half an eternity, it seemed, of toiling search.

It took me a long while to discover that other one. A long while. I felt I had swum through a light-year of mist, had fallen through the bottom of the Universe and had scrambled skyward to the sun itself. But I found him.

He was a definite shape before I had any chance to think of him, and when I thought him not there he still was there.

I had found him!

He was above me perhaps fifty feet and he seemed to be sitting on air and dangling his feet over the edge. Great gouts of mist rolled between us, blotting us from one another's sight. But each time the mist cleared, there we were again. I could not contain myself for joy and he seemed to feel much the same way, for he waved his arms down at me and beckoned me up. I beckoned him to come down. We must have been farther apart than it seemed to our eyes, for he could not hear me nor I him.

He was evidently frightened to let go of his perch in air and so I had to take the initiative. I looked along the way from me to him and thought hard about a stair. And step by step the stair appeared. I ran up it, shouting at him the while, but, in my enthusiasm, I forgot the stair and it vanished.

I landed as soon as I was frightened of earth's impact and

again built the stair. This time I looked at the steps as I went up and this time I arrived.

He was a diminutive fellow with a face which attested to a belligerent turn of mind. And his first greeting to me was, "Did you do all this?"

"No. George Smiley did it."

"Who?"

"George Smiley."

"Must have been an Earthman. I am from Carvon myself."

"Never heard of that," I said.

"Well, it *was* a nice place. I was researching on the regime of Vaso on Wwhmanin and all of a sudden my book vanished and here I was. And here I am."

"Here we both are," I said. "I've been looking all over for you. I need help. Did you see those stairs I just built?"

"Yes, but they're gone now. It wasn't such a good job."

"Well, I've discovered that all we have to do is think of something real hard and then it will come about. And if we can remember it—"

"If we can remember it. I've been trying to concentrate on a ham sandwich for a day and a half, but I keep forgetting it before I can eat it. Woops. There it goes again."

"Now look," I said. "I'll think about it, too."

"No, let's get something to sit on first. I don't know what's under me and I don't—"

"Don't say that!" said I, barely saving him from falling. "All right, we'll think of a table. There! There's a table. Now you keep thinking about that table while I get a couple of chairs—"

He shut his eyes and kept a grip on the table. I shut mine

and imagined us sitting on chairs. And then there we were, sitting on chairs—

"It's gone!" he said. And sure enough, the table was gone again. We had thought too hard about chairs. Finally we managed to feel natural and remember chairs and think of the table, too, and so, with some relief, we alternated thinking about things until we had something to eat and drink. But the trouble was that each time we would take a bite of something we would forget about the table and the food would plummet out of sight.

Somehow we filled up and then, looking thoughtful, he said, "You know, if we could just get practiced enough to think about all sorts of things, you and I, we could build the world back just about the way we want it. But the first thing we've got to do is to put the sun in the sky. I'm sick of this murk!"

"All right," said I, "I'll think about the sun."

And the sun shone brightly down. I must have been fairly well in practice, for I kept on talking and kept the sun up there at the same time.

"Now you think of Earth," I said.

He thought about Earth and a sort of uneasy motion was set up under us and flashy bits of scenery popped into view and vanished and popped up again. Chinese tombs and a far-off domed city and a ferryboat on a lake all appeared and disappeared.

"It's not much use," he said. "It just can't be done all at once. Let's imagine one town and then, when we get used to that and believe in it, we'll imagine the fields around it—"

"All right. But we really ought to imagine something to

build the town on. A great globe in the sky, twenty-five thousand miles in circumference—"

"Let's be different," he said suddenly. "As long as you and I can do this all by ourselves, we'll just put this together on some new principles. There's no use copying what we've already had. Now how about living inside the earth—" He stopped in awe. "Why, we—"

I cried, "Why . . . why, we're—"

"Yes," he said, "yes, we're—"

Oh, no, gentlemen," said a silkily sardonic voice. And we both whipped around to find George Smiley standing there in his flashtex cape. "If there is anything to be built, then I shall build it. You two are the most stubborn of all, but you've agreed with each other. And now you can agree with me.

"I worked for years to sell the world the idea of nonexistence. And if anyone intends to build a world then it shall be me. Who put that sun in my sky?" And he waved his hand toward it and the sun went out.

"We've got a perfect right," said my friend.

"No, you have not," grinned George Smiley. "I faded all things into nothingness, even Time, for myself. And because I made the whole world believe and all the Universe, then the Universe is mine. And I shall build."

"Why, you're trying to set yourself up as—"

"Yes," said George Smiley to my friend. "Yes, indeed."

"We have just as much right!" howled my friend.

"I shall then give you half of it," said George Smiley. "The lower, hotter half. I shall create a world for you alone to rule."

29

"No!" protested my friend.

"Yes," said George Smiley. "It's a quaint idea I got out of an old book. Now begone, both of you!"

And suddenly we were falling again. But this time no matter how much ground I thought about, no ground was there to stay me. My friend was soon separated from me and he did not see the water which suddenly spread below me. I know he did not, for he was still falling when last I saw him.

As for myself, I climbed out on a muddy bank of the Seine and wrung the water out of my clothes.

The United States Marines didn't even ask me any questions when they locked me in their jail as a possible enemy airman.

And I didn't volunteer any answers.

I was too glad not to have to think about that bunk before I stretched out upon it.

George Smiley can have the Universe for all I'll ever care.

A Can of Vacuum

A Can of Vacuum

BIGBY OWEN PETTIGREW reported, one fine August day, to the Nineteenth Project, Experimental Forces of the Universe, United Galaxies Navy, and was apparently oblivious of the fact that ensigns, newly commissioned out of the civilian UIT and utterly ignorant of military matters, were not likely to overwhelm anyone with the magnificence of their presence.

The adjutant took the orders carelessly and as carelessly said his routine speech: "Space Admiral Banning is busy but it will count as a call if you leave your card, Mr. Pettigrew."

Bigby Owen Pettigrew chewed for a while on a toothpick and then said: "It's all right. I'll wait. I got lots of time."

The office yeoman stared and then carefully restrained his mirth. The adjutant looked carefully at Pettigrew. There was a lot of Pettigrew to look upon and the innocent-appearing mass of it grinned a friendly grin.

The adjutant leaned back. The Universal Institute of Technology was doubtlessly a fine school so far as civilian schools went and it indubitably turned out very good recruits for the science corps. But this wasn't the first time that the adjutant had wished that a course in naval courtesy and law could be included there. The practical-joking Nineteenth would probably take this boy apart, button by stripe and cell by hair. Obviously Pettigrew really thought an ensign could call on a space admiral just like that.

"Perhaps," said the adjutant, "you have some important recommendations to make concerning the way he's running the project."

Pettigrew shook his head solemnly, all sarcasm lost upon him. "No. Just like to get the lay of the land, kind of."

"Are you sure," said the adjutant, "that you haven't some brilliant new theory you'd like to explain to him? Perhaps a new hypothesis for nebula testing?"

With a calm shake of his head, Pettigrew said, "Shucks, no. I'm away behind on my lab work."

The yeoman at the side desk was beginning to turn deep indigo with strangling mirth and managed, only at the last instant, to divert guffaws into a series of violent sneezes.

"You got a cold?" said Pettigrew.

The poor yeoman floundered out, made the inside of Number Four hangar and there was found some ten minutes later, in a state of aching exhaustion, by several solicitous mates who thought he had been having a fit. He tried for some time to communicate the cause of all this. But his mates did not laugh. They looked pityingly at him.

"Asteroid fever," said one.

"Probably got a columbar throngustu, poor fellow."

"Looks more like haliciticosis," said a third, vainly trying to feel the yeoman's pulse.

"All right," said the yeoman. "All right. You're a flock of

horse-faced ghouls. You wouldn't believe your mother if she said she was married! Doubt it! But he's here, I tell you. And that's what he did. And you mark my words, give that guy ten days on this station and none of you will ever be the same again."

The yeoman spoke louder and truer than he knew.

Carpdyke, the sad and suffering project assignment officer, who felt naked when he went to dinner without a couple of exploding cigars and a dematerializing pork chop, leaned casually up against the hangar door. The enlisted men had not seen him and they jumped. When they saw it was Carpdyke, they jumped again, further.

"What," said Carpdyke, "did you say this young gentleman's name was?"

"Pettigrew," said the yeoman, very nervous.

"Hmmm," said Carpdyke. "Well, men, I'm sure you have work to do." He was gloomy now, the way he always got just before he indulged his humor.

The group disappeared. Carpdyke went sadly back to his office and sat there for a long, long time. He might have been studying the assignment chart. It reached twelve feet up and eighteen feet across and was a three-dimensional painting of two million light-years of Universe. Here and there colored tacks marked the last known whereabouts of scout ships which were possibly going about their duties collecting invaluable fuel data and possibly not.

Carpdyke grew sadder and sadder until he looked like a bloodhound. His chief raymaster's mate chanced to look up, saw it and very, very nervously looked down. Just what was coming, the chief knew not. He hoped it wasn't coming to him. Carpdyke had been known to stoop so low as to rig a bridegroom's quarters with lingerie the morning of the wedding. He had even installed Limburger cheese in a spaceship's air supply. And once—well, the chief just sat and shuddered to recall it.

The door opened casually and Bigby Owen Pettigrew, garbed newly in a project-blister-suit-less-mask, the fashion there on lonely Dauphiom where beards grew in indirect proportion to the number of women, entered under the cloud of innocence.

The chief looked at Carpdyke, at Pettigrew and then at Carpdyke again. The assignment officer was growing so sad that a tear trembled on one lid. The chief stopped breathing but then when no guardian angel snatched Pettigrew away from there, the chief started again. No reason to suffocate.

"Hello," said Pettigrew cheerfully.

"You're new here, aren't you?" mourned Carpdyke.

"I just graduated from the UIT," said Pettigrew. "My name's Bigby. What's yours?"

"I'm Scout Commander Carpdyke, Bigby. We always like to see our new boys happy with the place. You like your hangars?"

"Oh, sure."

"You found the transportation from the Intergalaxy comfortable and prompt?"

"Sure, sure."

"And your room? It has a lovely view?"

"Well, now," said Pettigrew thoughtfully, "I don't think I noticed. But don't you bother yourself, Commander. It suits me. I don't want much."

The chief was beginning to have trouble swallowing. He went to the water cooler.

"Well, now," said Carpdyke, looking very, very mournful, "I am happy to hear that. But you're sure you wouldn't want me to change quarters with you?"

"Change? Shucks, Commander, that's awful nice of you but—well, no. My quarters suit me fine and no doubt you're used to yours."

The chief sprayed water over the assignment map, dived straight out the door and kept going. A ululation of indescribable pitch faded away as he grew small across the rocket field.

"Did he get sick or something?" asked Pettigrew.

"A bit touched, poor man," said Carpdyke. "Ninety missions to Nebula M-1894."

"Poor fellow," said Pettigrew. But he braced up under it. "Now, then, Commander, is there anything you want me to solve or fix up? Anything you're stuck on or deep-ended with? They put me through the whole ten years and I sure want to do well by the service." He burnished a bit at the single jag of lightning on his lapel which made him an ensign, science corps, experimental.

"How were things at base? You left Universal Admiral Collingsby well, I presume."

"Sure, sure," said Pettigrew. "Read me my oath himself."

"You and ten thousand other plebes by visograph," muttered Carpdyke.

"Beg pardon?"

"Nothing. Nothing. I was just wondering where we could best use your services, Pettigrew. We have to be careful. Don't want to waste any talent, you know."

"Sure not! I bet you have an awful time keeping up with problems, huh?" Vivid excitement manifested itself on Pettigrew's homely face for the first time.

"There," said Carpdyke, "you have struck it. Keeping up. Keeping up. Ah, the weariness of it. Pettigrew, I'll wager you have no real concept of what we're up against here at Nineteen. Mankind fairly hangs on our reports, sir."

"I'll bet they do," said Pettigrew with enthusiasm.

"Here we are," said Carpdyke, "located in the exact hub of the Universe; located for a purpose, Pettigrew. A Purpose! Every exploding star must be investigated at once. Every new shape of a nebula must be skirted and charted. Every dark cloud must be searched for harmful material. Pettigrew, the emanations of all the Universe depend upon us. Upon us, Pettigrew." And here he heaved a doleful sigh. "Ah, the weariness of it, the weariness."

"Sure now, Commander. Don't take it hard. I mean to help out all I can. Just you tell me what you want done—"

Carpdyke rose and convulsively gripped the ensign's hand. "You mean it, Pettigrew? You mean it truly? Magnificent! Absolutely magnificent!"

"Just you tell me," said Pettigrew, "and I'll do my best!"

Carpdyke's exultation gradually faded and he sank back. He slumped and then shook his head. "No, you wouldn't do that. I couldn't ask you to do that."

"Tell me," begged Pettigrew.

"Pettigrew," said Carpdyke at last, "I have to confess. There *is* a problem. I hate to ask. It's so difficult—"

"Tell me!" cried Pettigrew.

Carpdyke finally let himself be roused. Very, very sadly he said: "Pettigrew, it's the rudey rays."

"Just you . . . the what?"

"Rudey rays. Rudey rays! You've heard of them certainly."

"Well, now, Commander . . . I . . . uh . . . rudey rays?"

"Pettigrew, how long were you at UIT?" And Carpdyke put deep suspicion into it.

"Why, ten years, Commander. But— Rudey rays. Gosh, I didn't never hear of anything like them."

"Pettigrew," said Carpdyke sternly, "rudey rays might well be the foundation of a new civilization. They emanate. They expand. They drive. But they can't be captured, Pettigrew. They can't be captured."

"Well, what—?"

"A rudey ray," said Carpdyke, "is an indefinite particular source of inherent and predynamic energy, inescapably linked to the formation of new stars. Why, Pettigrew, it is supposed that the whole Universe might have been created from the explosion of just one atom made of rudey rays!"

"Gosh. I thought—"

"You thought!" cried Carpdyke. "Ah, these professors! They pour ancient, moldy and outmoded data into the hapless heads of our poor, defenseless young and then send them out—"

"Oh, I believe you," said Pettigrew. "It's just kind of sudden. A new theory, like."

"Of course," said Carpdyke, sadly but gently. "I knew you would understand. This matter is top secret. Nay, it is *bond* top secret. Pettigrew, if we had just one quart of rudey rays—"

"One what?"

"One quart!"

Pettigrew nodded numbly. "That's what I thought you said."

"Pettigrew, with just one quart of rudey rays we could run the United Galactic Navy for a million years at full speed. All five million ships of them. We could run the dynamos of all our systems for ten thousand years without stopping. And—"

Pettigrew was wide-eyed. "Yes?"

Carpdyke leaned closer, "Pettigrew, with just one quart of rudey rays, we could make a whole new universe."

Pettigrew fanned himself uncertainly.

"Good!" said Carpdyke. "I'll give you your orders." And before another word could be spoken he scrawled across a full page of the order blank:

TO ALL ACTIVITIES:

Ensign Bigby O. Pettigrew, pursuant to verbal orders this date to the effect that he is to locate, isolate and can one quart of rudey rays, is hereby authorized to draw necessary equipment on the recommendation of supply and laboratory commands.

Carpdyke

Carpdyke leaned closer, "Pettigrew, with just one quart of rudey rays, we could make a whole new universe."

With a flourish he gave it over. And with a hearty handshake and a huge smite upon the back, Carpdyke propelled the ensign to the door. Pettigrew was thrust out and the wind fluttered in the sheet he held. He looked at it, frowned a little and then, squaring his shoulders manfully, strode purposefully upon his way.

Behind him Carpdyke stood for a little while, devils flickering in his eyes and something like a smile on his mournful mouth. Then he sat down.

"The first thing supply will send him for is a can of vacuum," said Carpdyke. "I figure that should take him a couple of days. Then lab will want—" But he shook off these pleasures and looked moodily at his assignment blanks.

He'd have to have something new in three or four days. Pettigrew ought to be good for a solid month before he began to wise.

"Sir," said the chief raymaster's mate, "dispatches from base." He looked at them. "All routine."

"I'm busy," said Carpdyke, throwing them into the basket. He settled himself down to compound and compute the next mission of the luckless Pettigrew. "'Now, then, Commander,'" he mimicked, "'is there anything you want me to solve or fix up?'" He nearly chuckled. "Ah, Pettigrew, Pettigrew . . ." He grew mournful again and the chief looked very, very uncomfortable as time wore on.

"Sir," ventured the chief, "that top dispatch says a new batch of officers is being ordered in here. About fifteen ensigns, a couple of commanders and one captain, Congreve, to take over as exec. That's the Congreve that was cited for his work on new fuels. He'll probably make this place hot. I—"

"Shut up," said Carpdyke, "I'm busy." And to himself, "When he gets chased all over the post with that, we'll try pink beta rays and maybe a left-handed Geiger counter. Then—"

There was a stuttering snarl out in the hangar and heavy ground vibrations as a big motor warmed. The chief scowled. He looked at his assignment sheets and let off a couple of regulation growls.

"No flights due off for a week. What's wrong with them monkeys?" He went to the office door and stood there, a little blinded by the pink daylight. He saw a Number Thirty Starguide being dollied out by a tractor for a takeoff. It wasn't the space admiral's barge, but a routine mission cruiser. And the peculiar thing about it was, no lab crew standing by.

When they had the Starguide into position for its launch one lone figure came shuffling out, climbed the ladder and popped into the hatch. The tractor detached itself and the tower waved all clear.

There was something reminiscently all wrong about the man who had entered that ship and the chief was almost ready to turn away when it struck him.

"Pettigrew!" He started to run into the field and then realized his complete lack of authority. He dashed back.

Carpdyke was still absorbed.

"Sir!" said the chief. "That ensign got a ship! He's about to take off!"

Carpdyke almost said "I'm busy," and came alert and up instead. "Who?"

"Pettigrew got a ship. There!"

Carpdyke was stunned. He ran forward and then was slammed back into the door by the recoil blast of the Starguide. One moment there was a ship, the next there was the dust. Pettigrew was gone.

"You sure that was Pettigrew?" cried Carpdyke.

"I seen him."

Carpdyke breasted the flying clouds of dirt which lingered and got himself to Flight Operation.

He slammed inside. "What's going on? Who was in that ship?"

"Ensign Pettigrew," said the warrant dispatcher.

"What?" cried Carpdyke. "Where is Lieutenant Morgan?"

"Sick bay," said the warrant dispatcher. He had been scared for a moment but now he knew he was in the right. He was an old Navy man. An order was an order and he had the copy right there.

"Why did you let that man get away?"

"Sir," said the warrant, "I seen your order not ten minutes back. We was to lend every assistance to Ensign Pettigrew. Well, we did!"

Carpdyke was keeping upright by holding the edge of the signal rack. A million dollars' worth of spacecraft, the life of a new officer— "But he . . . but that was just—" He caught hold of himself. "That order was intended to be seen by Morgan. The man was new."

"I got the duty," said the warrant doggedly, "and I obeyed it."

44

*Carpdyke was stunned. He ran forward and then was slammed
back into the door by the recoil blast of the Starguide.
One moment there was a ship, the next there was the dust.*

Carpdyke went away from there with a complete panorama of a twelve-man court-martial board staring him unsympathetically in the eye. What had he sent that fool after? Rudey rays. Knowing less than nothing about the fiery character of luminous masses, an ensign would burn himself to bacon crispness the first one he ran through. No ensign, no ship, no further career for Carpdyke.

He had no choice but to declare himself guilty. He went into the outer office of the admiral's suite and looked sadly at the adjutant. "Is he in?"

"Sure, but—"

Carpdyke went wearily by and breasted the barricades.

Banning was rather fat, somewhat crotchety, and had a most wary eye upon his future. He had managed to live twenty-one years with the Navy without sullying his record and if he could keep one more clean he would be pleasantly selected up by his friends to some post as galactic commander with the rank of sixteen stars. Today he was musing upon his happy future, making thoughtful steeples with his fingers and watching his favorite cat dozing in the daylight which poured in.

"Sir," said Carpdyke, remembering suddenly that he had forgotten his jacket and cap, "a new man, Pettigrew, just reported. An ensign. He was awful green and I sent him out with a funny order and Morgan is in sick bay today and his warrant obeyed the order and now Pettigrew and a million dollars' worth of Number Thirty Starguide are on their way someplace to get fried. I am turning in my resignation and will hold myself—"

Banning's eyes went round as he attempted to digest these facts. Then he ordered a repeat and when it had been carefully told four or five times with details, he suddenly understood that sixteen stars might very well eclipse if such things were found to have happened on his base.

"Order up the cruisers! Send out ten destroyers! Man the warning net!" bawled Banning. And then he grabbed his cap and sprinted for the radio room.

Carpdyke relayed the orders and within ten minutes, where peacefulness had reigned, great waves of motors began to beat and the ground quaked under the impact of emergency takeoff.

The men were not quite clear on what they were to do or where they were to go. And it took Banning several minutes on the shortwave to convince four or five irate commanders, who objected to leaving so fast, that they were not about to repulse a rebel attack.

Meanwhile a small, dark radioman was having no luck with Pettigrew. "Sir," he said to Banning, "he can't have any channels switched on. I've tried them all. And probably he's outraced even the ion beams by this time. I don't think—"

"Don't think!" cried Banning. "Don't ever think! Stop that ship!"

But nobody stopped that ship. For five standard days Banning's guard fleet raked and combed the surrounding space and then, because they had left without proper provisions, began to return one by one, each with negative news.

Carpdyke, miserable but not under arrest yet because Banning could not stop worrying long enough to think up the proper charges, wandered around the hangars. He received very little sympathy. Hardly anyone on the project had escaped Carpdyke's somewhat heavy wit and, combined with this, all crews present had gone without liberty or relief for a week. The project was very grim. The brig was full of people who hadn't saluted properly or had demonstrated negligence in the vicinity of Space Admiral Banning. Things were confused.

At least three times a day Banning picked up his pencil to send intelligence of this harebrained accident to the department and each time was stopped by his vision of those sixteen stars. He could court-martial Carpdyke, but then it would come out that Carpdyke was notorious and that Banning, being of the haze school himself, had never put a full astern on the practice. Banning was confused.

Ten days went by with no word of Pettigrew and out of complete weariness the project began to settle into an uncertain sort of routine. The chaplain left the bridge table long enough to inquire whether or not he should read an absentee burial for the young officer and was told off accordingly. Scout ships returning with routine data were ignored and immediately fell under the same gloom which was downing everyone else.

Nobody spoke to Carpdyke.

When the admiral spoke to anybody they got rayburns.

The post publicity officer began to write up experimental releases about another brave young martyr of science and the master-at-arms inventoried the scanty baggage of Pettigrew. People began to look worn.

And then, at four o'clock of a September day, a Number Thirty Starguide, rather singed around the edges and coughing from burned-out brakes, came to rest before Hangar Six and out popped a very secondhand version of Bigby Owen Pettigrew.

People stopped right where they were and stared.

"Hello," said Pettigrew.

But people just stared.

Admiral Banning had been soon told and was coming up puffing and scarlet. Carpdyke slithered out of his office and tried to seem as if he wasn't present.

"Hello, Mr. Carpdyke," said Pettigrew.

"Young man!" said Banning. "Where have you been?"

"Are you Admiral Banning?" asked Pettigrew.

"Answer me!"

"Well, I guess I been all around, mostly. I scouted about three nebulas and almost lost the whole shooting match in the last one, what with the emissions and all. And I got pretty shaken up with the currents and reversed fields and—"

"What was the idea taking off that way?" cried Banning.

"Well, Mr. Carpdyke, he told me to go out and get a quart of rudey rays and I—"

"A quart!" cried Banning.

"Yes, sir. Seemed kind of funny to me, too. But he said these rudey rays was the germs of new universes so I—"

"Rudey rays!"

"No, sir, I never heard of them either, Admiral. But orders is orders, so I went out—"

"You young fool! You might have been killed! You might have lost that ship!"

"Admiral," said Pettigrew, "that's just the way it seemed to me, too. But when he said how powerful these rudey rays was, why, I recollected when I was flying the Mail—"

"What mail? I thought you were a UIT man!" said Banning.

"Oh, sure, I am, sir. But five or six years before that I was flying the Empire Mail. Then when I found that new fuel you're using, they give me a scholarship to UIT which was mighty nice because back in Texas I never got much formal learning. And after I'd done some work on star clusters they said was new, why, I wanted to get back to flying again, so I figured this was the place to be. I ain't much of a hand about the Navy—"

This startling dissertation was abruptly punctured by the arrival of a cruiser which slammed down smartly enough to knock out a couple of windowpanes.

From it stepped a splendid young captain who approached the waiting group and saluted the admiral.

"Captain Congreve, sir, reporting to relieve the exec. I— Oh, hello, Pettigrew!"

There was so much warmth in Congreve's voice that Banning was startled.

"You know this man?" cried Banning.

"I certainly do. And I can recommend him to you heartily," said Congreve. "Picked him myself after Universal Admiral Collingsby swore him in. He invented the billion-light-year fuel capsule. You've heard of him, haven't you? Well, you must have: I see you've been on a mission already."

"Yes, sir," said Pettigrew. "I was sent off to get a quart of rudey rays."

"A . . . a what?"

"And I got 'em," said Pettigrew, pulling a flat jar from his sagging jacket. "Had quite a time and near got sizzled but they're tame enough. I saturated sponge iron with them and the filings are all here. Kind of a funny way to carry the stuff but I guess you Navy guys know what you are doing."

"Rudey rays?" said Banning.

"Thousand-year half-life," said Pettigrew, "and completely harmless. Good brake fuel. Won't destroy grass. By golly, Mr. Carpdyke, it was awful smart of you to figure these things out. They ain't in any catalogue and I sure didn't know they existed."

Technicians passed the flask from hand to hand gingerly. The counters on their wrists sang power innocuous to man and sang it loud.

"That's all I could get this trip. Nebula One, right slam bang center of the Universe," said Pettigrew. "Well, there she is. If you'll excuse me, I don't look much like a naval officer and I better change my clothes."

They stared after him as he went to quarters, the master-at-arms trotting after to break out his impounded gear.

There was a queer dazed look about Carpdyke. But Banning was not dazed. He fired some fast, smart questions at the technicians and when they had examined the fuel in the lab, they gave him some pretty positive answers.

Banning stood looking at Carpdyke, then, but not seeing him. Banning was seeing sixteen stars blazing on the side of a flagship and maybe not a whole year away after all.

"Sir," stammered Carpdyke, "I'm sorry. It came out all right but I know I jeopardized equipment. He looked so young and green and I figured it would take a lot of roasting to make him an officer and I never intended he would actually get off the base—"

Captain Congreve looked mirthfully at Carpdyke, for the captain understood the situation now.

"Commander," said Congreve, "I wouldn't let this throw you. You see, the reason Collingsby swore that man in as an ensign and not as a lieutenant was because Pettigrew had something of a reputation in the Empire Mail."

"A reputation?" said Carpdyke.

"Yes," said Congreve, gently. "A reputation as a practical joker, Commander, and he'd been warned about you."

"A pract . . . a practical—" began Carpdyke, feeling most ungodly faint at what this would do to his reputation everywhere.

"Carpdyke," beamed Banning, clapping him on the shoulder in a most friendly, sixteen-star-blinded way, "supposing we all go over to the club and let you buy us a drink?"

240,000 Miles
Straight Up

CHAPTER ONE

Left at the Post

THE party was wild. The night was gay. And the "Angel" was very, very drunk.

But who wouldn't have got drunk on such an occasion? The Angel was about to head man's first attempt to conquer space and within a few short hours he would be boring space to the moon, 240,000 miles straight up.

He had tried to stay sober but this, being without precedent in the Angel's career, was entirely too great a strain. "Don't dare take another grink . . . well . . . jush one more . . . *hic!*"

The Angel was First Lieutenant Cannon Gray of the United States Army Air Forces, Engineers. He was five feet two inches tall and he had golden curly hair and a face like a choir boy. Old ladies thought him wonderful and beautiful. His superiors, from the moment he had entered West Point, had found him just about the wickedest, hard-drinkingest, go-to-hell splinter of steel they'd ever tried to forge.

The Army, with a taste of opposites, called him Angel from the first, called it to his face, loved him and was hilarious over his escapades.

This was probably the first time in history that Angel had attempted to stay sober. But it was a wonderful party they were giving in his honor (two floors of the Waldorf *plus* the ballroom) and people kept insisting that he wouldn't get another chance at a drink for months and maybe never and everyone was so pleasant that good resolutions were very hard to hold—especially for a dashing young officer who had never tried to make any before.

The occasion was gala and his hand was sore from being pumped by brass hats and newsmen and senators. For at zero four zero eight of the dawning, First Lieutenant Cannon Gray, USA, was taking off for the moon.

It was in all the papers.

Several times Colonel Anthony, a veritable old maid of a flight surgeon, had tried to pry his charge loose and steer him to bed and, while Angel seemed willing and looked blue eyed and agreeable, he always vanished before the hall was reached. Really, it was not Angel's fault.

No less than nineteen frail, charming and truly startling young ladies, all professing undying passion and future faithfulness, had turned up one after the other and it was something of a task making each one unaware of the other eighteen and confirming in her belief in his lasting fidelity.

Such strains should not be placed upon young men about to fly 240,000 miles straight up. And it takes hours to say a proper goodbye. And it takes more hours to be respectful to brass. And it takes time, time, time to drink up all the toasts shoved at one. All in all it was a very exhausting evening.

Not until zero one zero six did Colonel Anthony manage to catch the collapsing Angel in such a way as to keep him. Wrapped in the massive grip of Colonel Anthony, Angel said, "Candrin four oh eigh . . . *snore!*"

The golden head dropped on the Colonel's eagle and Angel slept.

Cruelly, it was no time at all before somebody was slapping Angel awake again, standing him on his feet, getting him into a uniform, wrapping him up in furs, weighing him down with equipment and generally tangling up a dark, dismal and thoroughly confused morning.

Angel was aware of a howling headache. Small scarlet fiends, especially commissioned by the Prince of Darkness for the purpose, played a gay chorus with red-hot hammers just behind Angel's eyes. He was missing between his chin and his knees and his feet wandered off on various courses.

A flight major and two sergeants, undeniably capped with horns, danced in high anxiety around him and managed to touch him in all the places that hurt.

He was in horrible condition and no mistake.

And the watch on his wrist gleamed as hugely as a steeple clock and said, "Zero three fifty-one," in an unnecessarily loud voice.

The corridor was at least half the distance to Mars and Angel kept hitting the walls. The casual chairs with which he collided all apologized profusely.

A potted palm fell on him and then became a general who, with idiotic pomposity said, "Fine morning, fine morning, Lieutenant. You look fit. Fit, sir. No clouds and a splendid full moon."

He felt the call, one which generals too old for command

57

can never resist, to give a young officer the benefit of a wealth of experience but, fortunately, his aide swiftly interposed.

The aide was brilliant with the usual aide's enthusiasm for paper glory and distaste for generals. Angel knew him well. The aide, in Angel's day at the Point, had been an upperclassman, a noted grind, a shuddery bore and the darling of his seniors. He didn't look any better to Angel this morning.

"Beg pardon, sir," said the aide sidewise to the general, "but we've just time to brief him as we ride down. Here, this way Lieutenant." And, abetted by the usherlike habit peculiar to the breed of aides, he got Angel into the car.

"Now," said the aide to Angel, who was hard put to stifle his groans and shivers at the unearthly hour, "you have been thoroughly briefed. But there must be a quick resumé unless you think you are thoroughly cognizant of your duties."

Angel would have answered but the sound came out as a groan.

"Very well," said the aide, just as though his were the really important job and Angel was just a sort of paperweight, very needful to aides but not at all important. "The staff is terribly interested in your surveys.

"You will confine yourself wholly to this one task. It has been thought wisest to entrust a topographer with this first mission because, after all, that's the way things are done. We've insufficient reconnaissance to send up a main body."

Angel would have added that he was a guinea pig. They didn't even know if he could really get to the moon. But aides talk like that and lieutenants somehow let them.

"As soon as you have completed a survey of an elementary

sort you will televise your maps, then send a complete set in a pilot rocket and return if you are able. But you are not to risk bringing the maps back personally."

They were little enough sure he'd ever get there, much less get back.

"You will phone all data back to us. Our tests show that the wave can travel much further than that. Anything you may think important, beyond maps and perhaps geology, you are permitted to note and report.

"Under no circumstances are you to attempt to change any control settings in your ship. Everything is all prenavigated and proper setting will be phoned to you for your return.

"All instructions are here in this packet."

Angel shoved the brown envelope into his jacket and felt twinges of pain as he did so.

"My boy," said the general, getting a word in there somehow, "this is a glorious occasion. You have been chosen for your courage and loyalty and it is a great honor. A great honor, my boy. You will, I am sure, be a credit to your country."

Angel didn't mean it to be a groan but that is the way it came out. They had chosen him because he was the smallest man ever to enter West Point, his height having been waived because of the lump of tin—the Congressional Medal of Honor, no less—he had won as an enlisted man (under age) in the war.

They had needed a topographer who wouldn't subtract from payload. Space travel was to begin with seeming to create a demand for a race of small men. But he didn't tell the general this and they came to the end of the ride.

The aide expertly ushered Angel out into the bleak blackness of the takeoff field, where every officer and newspaperman who could wangle it was all buttoned up to the ears and massed about the whitish blob of the ship.

The flight surgeon took over, and protected Angel from the back swats and got him through to the ladder. The two smallish master sergeants—Whittaker and Boyd—were waiting at the top in the open door of the ship. Metal glinted beyond them in the lighted interior.

Whittaker was methodically chewing a huge wad of tobacco and Boyd was humming a bawdy tune as he stared up at the romantically round and glowing moon in the west. They were taking off away from it for reasons best known to the US Navy navigators who had set the course.

A commander was hurrying about, muttering sums, and he paused only long enough to glare at Angel. "Don't touch those sets!" he growled, and rushed off to take station at the pushbutton which, when all was well, would fire the assist rockets under the carriage on the rails. These were keyed in with the ship's rockets. The commander glared at his ticking standard chronometer.

The flight surgeon said, "Well, you've got a week to sober up, boy. You won't like this takeoff."

Angel gave him a green smile. It hadn't been the champagne. It was the apricot cordial that Alice had brought him to take along. "I'll be fine," said Angel, managing a ghost of his lovely smile.

"*Board!*" shouted the commander.

Angel went up the ladder. Whittaker spat out his chaw and lent a hand. Boyd was standing by on the stage and, more to avert the necessity of having to see Angel's poor navigation than from interest, turned a powerful navy night glass on the moon. Boyd was very fond of Angel in a cussing sort of way.

But Angel made it without help and had just turned to give the faces, white blurs there in the floodlights, a parting wave to the click of cameras when Boyd yelled.

"Oh, my aching aunt!"

There was so much amazed fear in that shout that everyone stared at Boyd and then turned to find what he saw. Angel found Boyd shoving the glasses at him.

"Look, Lieutenant!"

Angel hadn't supposed himself able to see a thousand-dollar bill, much less the clear moon. And then he jumped as if he'd been clipped with a bullet.

The commander was howling at them to batten down but Angel stood and stared, glasses riveted to the lunar glory.

Those with sharper eyes could see it now. And a wail went up interspersed with awful silences. Even the testy commander turned to stare, looked back to the ship and then whipped about to snatch a quartermaster's glass from his gunner. He took one look and froze in silence.

Every face was uplifted now, the field was stunned. For there on the moon in print which must have been a hundred miles high, done in lampblack, were the letters—

USSR

CHAPTER TWO

Takeoff

FOR some days Angel languished in bachelor officers' quarters, all out of gear. He had been nerved up to a job and then it hadn't come off. The frustration resulted in lack of any desire for animation of whatever kind.

It was the sort of feeling one gets when he says goodbye, goodbye, to all his friends at the curb and then, just as he starts off in the car, runs out of gas and has to call a garage.

His room was littered with newspapers which he had long since perused. The messboy brought stacks in every now and then until bed and furniture seemed to be constructed badly of newsprint.

His own personal tragedy was such that he hardly cared for the details. Instead of being the first man to fly to the moon he was again just a simple lieutenant with nothing more than his deserved reputation for angelic wickedness. It came very hard to him, poor chap.

But it came very hard to the world as well. For events had transpired which made any former event, including World War II, a petty incident.

The world had been conquered without firing any other shots than those needed to propel Russian forces to the moon. The head of the Russian state had promptly issued manifestos in no uncertain terms demanding that all armies and navies be scrapped everywhere and Russian troops admitted as garrisons to every world capital. Russia had plans.

One by one countries had begun to fly the hammer and sickle without ever seeing a single Red army star.

For it was obvious to everyone. Even statesmen. All Russia had to do was launch atom bombs from the moon at any offender to destroy him wholly.

The mystery of how Russia had solved the atom bomb and had so adroitly manufactured all the plutonium it could ever need was solved when a Russian scientist stated for the press that he had needed but one year and the Smyth report. Everybody began to quiet down, for at first there had been talk of traitors and selling the secret.

But now that it was at last obvious that there never had been any secret and that self-navigating missiles could be very easily launched from the moon at any Earth target and that, such was the gravity difference, it would be nearly impossible to bomb-saturate the moon from Earth, even the diehards could see they were whipped.

A demand on Washington had come from Russia for the entire US atom stockpile and Congress was debating right now, without much enthusiasm, a law to give it up.

It had been very striking the way the morale of the world had collapsed, seeing up there in the sky those giant letters, USSR. Communists in every land had begun to crawl out from under dubious cover and prepare welcomes for Russian troops (and the Russians had been bidding the foreign communists to crawl right back again).

To understate the matter, there was some little consternation in the nations and peoples of the world. And whatever labor thought about it they at least remembered that of all the civilized nations of Earth, Russia had been the only one after World War II to employ, use, exploit (and let die) slaves.

And then, just as surrender was being accomplished, the US Naval Intelligence working with the State Department had done some interception and unscrambling and decoding which again gave everyone pause. By great diligence and watchfulness they had managed to tap in on the Moscow-moon circuit to discover that all was not well.

Angel had been reading about the moon commander. The man was General Slavinsky and at first reading Angel had decided, with a bitterness not usually found in celestial sprites, that he hated the triply-damned intestines of General Slavinsky.

Slavinsky was known as the "Avenger of Stalingrad" and had been a very popular general in his own country. The Germans, however, had not liked him, jealous no doubt of the thorough sadism of the Russian.

When Slavinsky had not been winning battles he had been butchering prisoners and he had turned his men loose to loot in many a neutral town and conquered province. Slavinsky evidently had himself all mixed up with Genghis Khan, complete with pyramids of skulls.

The pictures in the papers showed Slavinsky to be a big, powerful man, meticulously uniformed, always smoking cigarettes. Typical corporal-made-good, Slavinsky had been Moscow's favorite peasant. About as cultured as a bull, he was quite proud of his refinement. And he had been sent with troops, supplies and bombs to command Russia's most trusted post, the moonbase.

It was here that dictatorship displayed its weakness. Bred by force out of starvation, the Russian state had very scant background of tradition. And trustworthy military forces are trustworthy only by their tradition. Slavinsky owed no debt to anyone but the Russian dictator. The Russian people would not know one dictator from another.

It developed, when Slavinsky was well dug in, that he had been a Trotskyite since boyhood and the murder of his ideal in Mexico had left him festering very privately. At least that was a fine excuse.

Once there Slavinsky began to make certain demands on Moscow. Moscow was beginning to be acrimonious about it. The dictator had ordered Slavinsky home and Slavinsky had told the dictator where he could stuff Moscow. Moscow was now threatening to withhold needed supplies.

US Naval Intelligence and the State Department were very interested and rumors flew amongst the personnel of the US moon expedition that something was about to break.

Angel lay on his back, feet against the wallpaper and gloomed. When a knock came on the door he supposed it was another load of papers and sadly said, "Come in."

But it was a colonel who stood there and Angel very hastily bounced up to sharp attention.

"We're having callers, son," said the colonel. "Be down in the court in five minutes."

Disinterestedly, Angel got himself into a blouse and

wandered out. He wondered if he would ever feel human and normal again. All his life he had been a somewhat notorious but really rather unimportant runt and the big chance to be otherwise had passed, it seemed, forever.

He hardly noticed his fellow officers as he lined up in the court. Most of them were of the moon gang, destined to go, once upon a time, in various capacities on the abandoned expedition. None of them looked very cheerful.

There was hardly a ripple or a glance when the big Cadillac drew up at the curb. Their senior barked attention and the officers drew up. Only then, when ordered to see nothing and be a robot, did Angel note that the car had the SECNAV's flag on it.

Four civilians, namely the secretary of state, the secretaries of defense, war and the Navy, alighted, followed by a five-star admiral and a five-star general. They were a dispirited group and they cast wilted glances over the lines of young officers.

The colonel in command of the detachment fell in with them behind the secretary of state and proceeded with this strange inspection.

Finally the group drew off and stood beside the Cadillac talking in low tones until they nodded agreement and then waited.

The colonel sang out, "Lieutenant Gray!"

Angel started from his trance, came to attention, paced front and center and automatically saluted the group. The colonel looked baffled as he came forward.

In a voice the others could not overhear, the colonel said, "I have no idea why they chose you, Angel. They were looking specifically for the tamest officer here. God knows how or why, but you won. They couldn't have looked at the records!"

"Thank you, sir," said Angel.

The colonel gave him a hard look and led him off to the car.

They didn't say anything to him. Angel got in beside the driver, and, when the doors had shut behind the rest, they moved off at a dispirited speed.

Nothing was said until they arrived in the driveway of the White House and then the general told Angel to follow them.

The abashed lieutenant alighted on the gravel, looked up at the big hanging lantern and the door, then quickly went after his superiors. This was all very deflating stuff to him. The closest he had ever come to the president was leaving his card in the box for the purpose in the Pentagon Building—and he doubted that the president ever read the cards dropped by officers newly come to station or passing through.

He hardly saw the hall and was still dazed when the general again asked his name, sotto voce.

"Mr. President," said the five star, "may I introduce First Lieutenant Cannon Gray."

Angel shook the offered hand and then dizzily found a chair like the rest. All eyes were on him. Nobody was very sure of him, that was a fact. Nobody liked what he was doing.

"Lieutenant Fay—" began the president.

"Gray, sir."

"Oh yes, of course. Lieutenant Gray, we have brought you here to ask you to perform a mission of vital importance to your country. You may withdraw now without stigma to yourself when I tell you that you may not return from this voyage.

"We considered it useless to ask for volunteers since then we would have had to explain a thing which I believe we all agree is the most humiliating thing this country has ever had to do. We are not prepared just now for publicity. You may withdraw."

This, thought Angel, was a hell of a way to force a guy into something. Who could withdraw now? "I am willing," he said.

"Splendid," said the president. "I am happy to see, gentlemen, that you have chosen a brave officer. Here are the dispatches."

Angel looked through them quickly and then at the first page of the sheaf, which was a brief summary.

He learned that one Slavinsky, late general of Russia, had finally forever parted company with his dictator and had declared himself master of Russia *and* the world. The United States was now addressed in uncompromising fashion by Slavinsky and ordered to do two things.

One, immediately to prepare a land, sea and air attack on Russia—one city in the United States or one city in Russia to pay for the first use of atom bombs by either—in order to secure the government of that nation to Slavinsky. And two, to send instantly a long list of needed supplies by one of the spaceships known to be ready in the United States. Angel knew that he was to be interested in "two."

"This situation," said the president, "is unparalleled." And with that understatement, continued, "Unless we comply we will lose all our cities and still have to obey. We are insufficiently decentralized to avoid these orders.

"Humiliated or not, we must proceed to save ourselves. Slavinsky holds the moon and is armed with plentiful atom rockets. And he who holds the moon, we learn too late, controls all the Earth below.

"We are asking you," he continued, "to take the supplies to the moon. We have secretly loaded a spaceship with the required items and need only one officer and two men as crew.

"The reason we send you at all is to ensure the arrival of the supplies in case of breakage on the way and, more important, in the hope that Slavinsky will let you go and you can bring back data which, if accurate enough, may possibly aide us to destroy Slavinsky and his men."

"Mr. President," said the secretary of state, "we have chosen this man not for valor but for reliability. I think it was our intention that whoever we sent should attempt no heroics which would anger Slavinsky. I think Lieutenant May should be so warned."

"Yes, yes," said the president. "This is of the utmost importance. You are only to return *if* Slavinsky permits it. You are to attempt no heroics. For if you failed in them we would pay the price. Am I understood in that, Lieutenant?"

Angel said he was.

"Now then," said the president, "the spaceship is waiting and, when you have picked your two crewmen and Commander Dawson gives the word, you can leave. These dispatches"—and he took up a sheaf of them—"are for General

Slavinsky and may be considered important only as routine diplomatic exchanges."

Angel took the package and stood up.

"One thing more," said the admiral. "You will be carrying a small pilot rocket aboard. You will take the rolls from the automatic recording machines, place them in it just before you reach the moon and launch the missile back to Earth before landing. If we have enough data, though it is a forlorn hope, we may someday fight Slavinsky."

"I doubt it," said the secretary of state, "but I won't oppose your thirst for data, admiral."

They shook hands with the president and then Angel found himself back in the Cadillac, rolling through the rush-hour traffic of Washington. Soon they made it to the Fourteenth Street Bridge and went rocketing into Virginia to a secret takeoff field.

"Could you get me master sergeants Whittaker and Boyd?" said Angel timidly to the general.

"I'll have them picked up on the way by the barracks," said the general. "No word of this to anyone though."

"Yes, sir," said Angel.

When darkness had come at the secret field Commander Dawson turned up with a briefcase full of calculations from the US Naval Observatory and began to check instruments.

"Two o'clock," he told the general.

"Two o'clock," said the general to Angel.

Angel walked out of the hangar and joined Whittaker and Boyd.

Whittaker spat reflectively into the dust. "I shore miss the brass band this time, Lootenant."

"And the dames," said Boyd. "Boy, how I'd like me a drink. We got time to go to town, Lootenant?"

Angel was walking around in small circles, his beautiful face twisted in thought. Now and then he kicked gravel and swore most unangelically.

They were handing Slavinsky the world, that was that. And without a scrap. The slaughter of a Russian war was nothing to anyone compared to the loss of Chicago. Maybe it was logical but it just plain didn't seem American to be whipped so quick.

Suddenly he stopped, stared hard at Boyd without seeing him and then socked a fist into his palm.

"What's the matter?" said Boyd.

Angel went into the hangar where the big ship was getting ready to be rolled out on the rails now that her loading was done.

"General," said Angel, "as long as I may never have the chance again—and being young makes it pretty hard—you might at least let me go to town and buy a couple quarts for the ride up."

"You know the value of secrecy," warned the general. And then more kindly, "You can take my car."

Angel stood not. Some fifty seconds later the Cadillac was heading for town at speeds not touched in all its life before.

Whittaker and Boyd, in the back seat, bounced and applied imaginary brakes.

"Listen, you guys," said Angel. "Your necks are out as much as mine"—he avoided two streetcars at a crossing and screamed on up toward "F" Street—"and I ought to ask your permission."

"We're going to take a load of food to Slavinsky on the moon. Very hush-hush, though the only one we've to keep secrets from now is Slavinsky. But I intend to make a try at knocking off that base. Are you with me?"

"Why not?" said Whittaker.

"Your party," said Boyd.

Angel drew up before an apartment house on Connecticut Avenue and rushed out. He was back almost instantly with a grip and considerable lipstick smeared on his cheek.

Boyd thought he heard a feminine voice in the darkness above calling goodbye as they hurtled away. He grinned to himself. This Angel!

Their next stop was before a drug store and Angel dashed in. But he was gone longer this time and seemed, according to a glimpse through the window, to be having trouble convincing the druggist. Angel came out empty-handed and beckoned to his two men.

Whittaker and Boyd walked in. A young pharmacist looked scared. There was no one else in the place.

Angel walked around behind the pharmacist. "Close the door," said Angel. Three minutes later the pharmacist was bound quite securely in a back closet.

Angel ransacked the shelves and loaded up a ninety-eight-cent bag. They turned out the lights and closed the door softly behind them and went away.

Twenty-one minutes later a young chemical warfare classmate of Angel's was hauled from the bosom of his family and after some argument and several lies from Angel permitted himself to be convinced by SECNAV's Cadillac and went away with them.

They halted at an ordnance depot in Maryland at eight-fifteen and the young chemist opened padlocks and finally, with many words of caution, delivered into Angel's hands three small flasks.

It was well before two when Angel and his men came back to the field. They alighted with their burdens and whisked them into the ship.

"Find that drink?" said the general indulgently.

"Yes, sir," said Angel.

"Good boy!" said the general, chuckling over having been young once himself. He had not missed the lipstick and had applied the school solution.

Commander Dawson was growling and snarling around the ship like a vengeful priest. Behind him came two quartermasters carrying the precious standard chronometer and spyglass.

"Better get aboard," said Dawson roughly. "And don't monkey with those instruments. We're almost ready." His scowl promised that it didn't matter to him what happened: *this* time he was going to get that rocket upstairs!

CHAPTER THREE

Moon Meeting

STARK death was the moon. No halftones, no softness. Black and white. Knife-edged peaks and sharp rills. Hot enough to fry iron. Cold enough to solidify air. Brutal, savage, dead. Strictly Mussorgsky.

A place you wouldn't want to go on a honeymoon, Angel decided.

For all of Dawson's growling they had not hit the target exactly. Slavinsky had drawn a big lampblack X below the USSR on a plateau near Tycho but the ship had hit nearly eight miles from it.

Hit was the word, for if they had not landed in pumice some thirteen feet thick things would have been dented. The abrasive dust had risen suddenly and drifted down with an unnatural slowness.

For a week they had been lying around in the padded cabin, experiencing spacesickness, worn out from accelerations and decelerations, living on K and D and C rations and cursing the engineers who had drawn such a thoroughly uncomfortable design.

Angel had sent off the pilot rocket as ordered, filled with the recording rolls, but he had added a few succinct notes of his own which he hoped the engineers would take to heart.

Such things as the way air rarefied up front on the takeoff and nearly killed Boyd.

Such things as drinking bottles that wouldn't throw water in your face when you got thirsty. Such things as straps to hold you casually down when your body began to wander around and helmets to keep your head from cracking against the overhead when you got up suddenly and found no gravity.

But for all the travail of the past week the Angel was bright-eyed and expectant. It was balanced off in his mind whether he would kill Slavinsky by slow fire or small knife cuts.

For Angel had very far from enjoyed being cheated of the glory of being the first man to fly to the moon and he distinctly disliked a man who would make a slave country of the United States. Prejudiced perhaps, but the Angel believed America was a fine country and should stay free.

Boyd raked up three packages, tying a line and a C-ration can, buoy-like, upon it. Whittaker got a port open, inside pane only, and looked at the scenery.

He turned and spat carefully into another can—experience had taught him, this trip—and then put on his space helmet, screwing the lucite dome down tight. He glanced at his companions.

Angel was having some trouble getting into his suit because of his hair, but when he had managed it he led the way to the space port. The three of them crawled over the supplies and entered the chamber, shutting the airtight behind them.

They checked their air supplies and then their communications. Satisfied, they let the outer door open. With a swoosh the air went out and they began their vacuumatic lives.

It was thirty feet down but they didn't use the built-in rungs. Angel stepped out into space and floated down like a miniature spaceship to plant his ducklike shoes deep into the soft pumice. Boyd followed him. Whittaker, carrying debris in the form of cans and bottles in his hugely gloved hands, came after.

As though on pogo sticks the three small ships bounced around to the rear of the spaceship. Boyd threw the three packages down and stamped them into the pumice. Whittaker scattered the debris around the one can which was the real buoy marker.

The discarded objects floated in slow motion into place and lay there in the deathly stillness.

They looked around and their sighs echoed in their earphones, one to the other. No tomb had ever been this dead.

They were landed in a twilight zone, thanks to Dawson. And if their suits—rather, vehicles—had not been so extremely well insulated they would already be feeling the cold.

The sky was ink. The landscape was a study in Old Dutch cleanser and broken basalt. A mountain range thrust startlingly sharp and high to the west. A king-size grand canyon dived away horribly to their south. A great low plain, once miscalled a sea, stretched endlessly toward Tycho.

Two miles away a meteor landed with a crash which made the pumice ripple like waves. A great column of the stuff, stiffly formed in an explosion pattern, almost stroboscopic, stood for some time, having neither gravity nor wind to disperse it.

A few fragments patted down, making new slow-motion bursts. But the meteor had landed at ten miles a second and they all winced and looked up into the blackness. Having atmosphere was a subtle blessing. Having none was horrible.

Looking up, Angel saw Earth. It was bigger than a Japanese moon and a lot prettier. It had colors, diffused and gentle, below its aura of atmosphere. It looked fairylike and unreal. Angel sighed and thought about his favorite bar.

They snowshoed around the ship again. The last of the sun, half visible like an upended saucer made of pure arc light, came to them through their leaded lucite helmets. That sun was taking a long, long time to set. Hours later it would still be sitting there. Things obviously took their time on the moon.

Whittaker, unable to spit, was having difficulties. Heroically, he swallowed his chew.

They weren't on the same wavelength with the Russians and the approaching detachment came within a quarter of a mile before they saw it. The group was tearing along, bouncing like a herd of kangaroos, sending up puffs of pumice at each leap. They came alongside the ship in a moment and, without any greeting to the newcomers, scrambled up inside.

The officer came back and peered out at the horizon and then ducked in again. It was very difficult to see through the metal helmets of these people but they looked hungry.

Angel went up and stood in the space door. The Russians had left the inner airtight open and all the atmosphere had rushed from the ship. Like madmen they were ripping at the boxes and stuffing chocolate and biscuit into their capacious bags. This was evidently personal loot and the way they were going at it looked bad for the boys who had stayed behind.

Nobody paid any attention to Angel, not even glancing his way, until the officer motioned Boyd and Whittaker into the ship and then unceremoniously herded the three of them into the forward hold and bolted a door on them.

Through a forward port Angel saw the two tractors approach. They were made of aluminum mostly, and they seemed to run out of a propane type tank. They threw hooks into the skids of the ship and, their huge treads soundlessly clanking, began to yank the ship toward the king-size grand canyon.

After an hour or so of tugging they came to the brink and were snaked around until they fitted on an oblong metal stage which, carrying tractors and all, promptly began to descend.

The ship lurched in the lower blackness and then lights flared up by which the stage could be seen to rise into place above them.

Eager crews of spacesuited men swarmed out of an airtight set in a blank wall and in a few moments a stream of supplies was being shuttled, bucket-brigade fashion, toward the entrance.

It was a weird ballet of monsters in metal. The supplies, so heavy on Earth, were tossed lightly from monster to monster which added to the illusion. Big crates of dehydrated sailed along like chips.

The unloading took three hours and eight minutes by Angel's watch and then the line cleared away. Belatedly somebody thought of the crew and unlocked the door. At pistol point they were rushed out, down the ladder and to the airtight. The gutted ship stood forlornly behind them, their only contact with home, associating now with six other monsters, the Stars and Stripes outnumbered.

In the dank corridor behind the second airtight, men were standing around in various stages of relaxation and undress. They kept halting to gloat over the supplies which left one Russian still in helmet but without pack or gloves, another stripped to underwear, a third in pack and all. Nobody glanced at them.

Their guard shoved them into another tunnel and they wound down a gentle grade between basalt walls until they came to another series of airtights. At the end they were shoved into a chamber walled all in metal, a sort of giant strongbox with doors at each of the five sides.

A desk made of packing boxes stood in the center. A rubber mattress bed was several feet behind it. A crude hat tree bore the fragments of a space suit. The place was a combination of arsenal, bedroom and office, sealed in, double-bolted, entrenched and triple-guarded.

At the desk sat a singularly dirty man, covered with matted black hair, clad in pants, glistening with perspiration and scowling furiously under crew-cut bristles.

This was Slavinsky, Vladimir, onetime general of Russia, currently dictator of the world.

The guard had got out of his clumsy space helmet. "The ship crew, Ruler," he said in English.

Whittaker had taken off his helmet and was biting at a plug of Ole Mule. Boyd was examining his fingernails.

Only Angel was still fully suited and helmeted.

"Who is commander?" barked Slavinsky, black eyes screwing up.

Boyd glanced up.

"I am Lieutenant Cannon Gray," he said with blue eyes wide.

"Don't forget the dispatches, Lootenant," said Whittaker.

Boyd tossed the packet on the desk. It floated down.

"I am displeased," said Slavinsky.

"I'm sorry to hear it," said bogus Gray. "I'll sure tell the president when I get back."

"You're not going back!" said Slavinsky. "You have failed."

"Looks to me like we brought a lot of supplies," said Boyd.

"You brought no cigarettes!" said Slavinsky.

"Well, if that ain't something," said Boyd. "I tell you them quartermasters ought to be horsewhipped and that's a fact. Well, well. No cigarettes. You sure you checked the inventory, general?"

"The title of address is 'Ruler'! And I'll have no questioning of our actions. You brought no cigarettes and there's not a single pack on the moon."

"Well, if it's okay with you," said Whittaker, "we'll just trot down and fetch you a couple cartons."

"That's impertinence! Lieutenant, have you no control over your men? Are you certain we have emptied all storage compartments of your ship?"

"Well, can't say. Back in the tube room we had a little layout for the return trip but you wouldn't want to take that away."

"Aha!" said Slavinsky, jumping up to his full five feet.

He pushed down a communicator button and rattled orders into it.

Just as he finished a small bespectacled man entered timidly, his hands full of reports. "Ruler, I have just checked the supplies and I find them safe. I began when the first case entered and have just finished. The food is not poisoned."

"So!" said Slavinsky to Boyd. "You knew better than to trip us up, did you. Ha!"

"I got to send my report to the president," said Boyd.

"I am afraid," said Slavinsky, "that I shall have to attend to that. Now, to business. You will be separated from your men, of course. And then men we need in our labor gangs. We have all too few men, you see.

"But you, as an officer, according to the usages of war, need not work outside but may have some light job. The meteors have been bad lately and we have lost several people. Guard, take this officer to a cell and put the men to work on the missile emplacements instantly."

"With a guard, Ruler?"

"No, blockhead. Where would they go? Ha, ha. Yes, indeed. Where would they go?"

Angel had been half through the act of unscrewing his helmet. Now he hastily replaced it. He and Whittaker were thrust outside and in a moment found themselves in the hands of a non-com who was organizing a work party.

A radio technician came up and adjusted their radios to proper wavelength and in a moment they were drowned in Russian.

Angel sighed with relief and looked back at the last of the doors which had led out from Slavinsky. Ruler of the world, was he?

Well, maybe he could manage to get some good out of it. But as for Angel, give him control over a bar stool of the Madrillon and Slavinsky could keep the moon.

Musing, he found himself in a column and outward bound.

CHAPTER FOUR

Wait for the Night

IT was still twilight on the surface and the earthlight was quite bright even where the blackness of airless night lay upon the stabbed and pitted world. The pumice-covered plains were upheaved into abrupt cliffs and slashed apart by ugly chasms.

It was a nightmare land where one bobbed in levitation-like gyrations, skating over soft and treacherous pumice bogs, plowing through the basalt dust of *rays,* all under an indigo sky.

Meteors landed soundlessly with the enormous explosions of bombs and each twenty-four hours millions fell. Sometimes clouds rose up to catch the higher rays of the slow-motion sun and hung there, twisting the light into colors.

Man was experiencing his first contact with the wild, garish, infinitely dangerous power of space, billions of times as strong, as capricious, as his ancient enemy the sea.

All was so slow, so quiet, so vastly untenanted. And far away the aura-crowned Earth hung silent, watchful in the sky, satellite of this dead world.

Their imperishable tracks stretched behind them as they drifted toward the emplacements. It was difficult to believe that these weird metal things were containers for human beings.

In ages to come, in scenes like these, men would sicken and madden and die just as the crews of tempest-driven barques have gripped insanity in the ages past.

Angel plowed through pumice and climbed the final bastion of the emplacement.

The great pilotless missile was shielded by an overhanging cliff against all but a freak meteor. Through a small opening this sleek white tube could fly, rushing to the execution of perhaps a million human beings. It stood quietly, waiting. It had all the dignity of the slave machine. It could wait.

Painted scarlet on its nose was—

CHICAGO

There was a buzz of cheerfulness from the Russians as they got out of the open. Eight of their number here had died—two from sun, one from cold, one from suffocation, four all at once under the smash of a thousand-ton meteor.

The mathematician amongst them sat down and began clumsy figures with his mitten-held pencil. A surveyor set up a transit. They were about to complete the orientation and construction of the rail tracks for Chicago.

Angel supposed he would remain here under guard. But the captain had ideas.

"You Yankees! There is rail material dumped in a small crater a few hundred yards from here. We have too few men as it is. You will begin the task of bringing them."

The ground vibrated for an instant as a meteor struck above.

Angel said, "Come on, Whittaker."

They crawled back over the entrance bulwark and regained the still twilight of the outside.

For a moment they stopped and adjusted the radio dials on each other's helmets.

"I hope Boyd is all right," said Angel.

"I hope we can find the place," said Whittaker.

They turned and in great leaps began to scout for the incoming tracks of their ship. There were many such tracks and Angel had to take a quick orientation. Then they found theirs, neither older nor younger than any other tracks, and began to race back down it, taking broadjumps of forty feet with every step, trying to keep from sailing sky-high. The pumice was indifferent footing and clung to their duck shoes, leaving a slowly settling stream of particles in the half-light behind them.

They had gone five miles before they saw anything on their backtrack. And then it was obvious that somebody in the work party had begun pursuit after missing them.

The pursuit was specklike, unhurried as the weasel stalks. For who could find board and room on the moon?

Angel's breath was hurtful in his lungs. Whittaker was lagging and the officer stopped to let him catch up. It was then he saw the motor sled. It was coming fast, so fast he could see it grow.

Desperately, Angel sprinted on. Ahead, with a yell of delight, he saw the end of the tracks and the strewn debris. He grabbed cans one after the other until he found the right one and hauled up its string. The first package came to light and then the string broke.

Whittaker dived headlong into the pumice to recover it. The second and third packages came to view.

Angel glanced back. The motor sled was almost there. He wrenched off the ties of the heaviest packet. Out rolled the sleek bombs of a bazooka and the instrument itself.

Whittaker seized the barrel and placed it over Angel's shoulder. Angel found the trigger and knelt, sighting on the sled. Whittaker thrust the first rocket in place.

The sled was quite close now, trying to brake, throwing up lazy clouds of pumice.

The rocket trail was red flame in the twilight. The explosion was soundless but like a blow on the chest. Scarlet fire sucked sled and men into its ball and then spewed them forth in fragments which fell lazily, driftingly through the clouds.

Angel got up and would have mopped his brow until his hand, striking against the helmet, reminded him where he was. He turned to find that Whittaker was already slinging the string of grenades over his shoulder.

From the third packet they took the Tommy guns and ammunition. Armed then and in haste they started the backtrack.

Had they been able to afford more oxygen they would not have been so tired. Weightless walking took little energy and their burdens were feathers. It was rather insecure to feel a Tommy gun so light.

They oriented themselves and then Angel led off toward the chasm. They gained the shelter of this just as a meteor seemed to explode behind them. But it wasn't a meteor. It was a rocket projectile of small caliber.

The explosion was soundless but like a blow on the chest.
Scarlet fire sucked sled and men into its ball and
then spewed them forth in fragments which fell lazily,
driftingly through the clouds.

They floundered down to a ledge in the giant canyon and then, like two mountain goats of great power, began to leap from outcrop to outcrop.

They made time. The canyon had a bend which would protect them until the last.

But Chicago was there.

A slug struck the bazooka barrel and glanced soundlessly away. They instantly pressed against a jagged break in the wall and Angel adjusted his burdens. He looked up and saw that he could climb.

With a motion to Whittaker to stay put, Angel went up the basalt and found himself crawling over an unburned meteor of glittery sheen. There were diamonds in it.

On top he could crawl forward and peer down over the edge at the Chicago rampart. He glanced ahead and saw that there were fifteen other emplacements but the main entrance to the tunnels interposed.

Cautiously he laid down his weapons and then crept to the edge again, grenades in hand.

With sudden rapidity he pulled out pin after pin and pitched. It was like salvo ranging. How hard it was to estimate throwing distances!

But the cliff wall let them billiard. One, two, three, four they dropped into the emplacement.

He could see space suits down there scrambling back. Any slightest wound would be fatal. A slug tipped his mitten and then the first grenade went up.

The emplacement rocked. Four blasts belched out stone. The imperfectly held rocks folded in and an avalanche began a leisurely curtain into the bottomless canyon. There was no sign of the Chicago entrance.

While particles still drifted, Angel waved to Whittaker and they swiftly resumed their goat travel. The huge steel faces of the main tunnels remained solid and impassive, proof even against meteors.

No shot came.

Whittaker cautiously drew up to their faces until he could touch them. He found no chink in them.

"Up!" said Angel.

They scrambled and leaped and finally came to the plain. A rocket missile shook the ground near them and covered them with dust. They dived headlong into a crater.

Whittaker lifted his head above the rim. "Emplacement to repel ground troops. On that crater rim."

"They must keep one manned continually as an alert," said Angel. He thoughtfully sat down. Somewhere a meteor shook ground. The tip of the last rocket explosion was still rising, catching the sunlight in a turning glitter.

"The only available entrance into the tunnels must be through that guarded emplacement," said Angel. He looked up. "There's very little sun left. It will be dark in half an hour."

Whittaker nodded inside his lucite casque. "It'll get awful dark, Lootenant."

"Fine," said Angel. "Take bearings on the emplacement from the two rims of the crater. A man could get hurt stumbling around here without lights."

Whittaker got busy with the engineer's companion, an

91

azimuth compass. It worked fairly well, though heaven knows where the magnetic pole of the moon might be. He made a small chart of prominent landmarks which would be easy to find in the dark.

Now and then a rocket would explode along the crater rim but such was the gravity problem that the alerts did not attempt the mortar effect.

Angel put a piece of chocolate into the miniature space lock of his helmet, closed the outer door, opened the inner one with his chin and worried it dog-fashion out of the compartment. He ate it reflectively.

"I hope Boyd is all right," he said.

CHAPTER FIVE

Now I Lay Me . . .

D ARK came as if someone had shut off an electric light in a coal cellar. The moment was well chosen. Dark wouldn't come in such a fashion to this place again for twenty-nine and a half days, nor would it be light again until half that period had passed.

Soon it would get very cold, down to minus two hundred centigrade. These space suits were designed for that but they used up their batteries very quickly despite the eight thicknesses of asbestos on their outsides.

"Let's go," said Angel. "They may try a foray on their own." The earthlight was wiped out by their colored helmets.

As nearly as they could calculate they covered the proper chart distances in a wide triangle which would bring them up the side of the alert post.

Soundlessly they made their debouch, fortunately having to take no care of tumbled meteor fragments beyond falling. And a fall was far from fatal.

They came to the slope and groped their way up.

Something round bumped Angel. He felt it and found it to be a metal pole. Some sort of aerial or light stand. He wondered if the Russians had shifted to other helmets which would permit them to see him in the earthlight. That he was still alive made him think not.

He felt the man-made smoothness of the pit edge and drew back. He stopped Whittaker and toothed out the pin of a grenade.

Rapidly they hurled four. The pumice shook like jelly under them under four explosions.

They dived over the edge. Only one Russian was there and nothing much of him was remaining.

"They tried a foray," said Angel. He threw on his chest lights and the metal escape door gleamed.

They lifted it swiftly and plunged down the steps, closing it behind them. An airlock was before them.

"Keep your helmet on," said Angel. He went through.

At the third door they paused and took the safeties off their Tommy guns. They went through alertly. But no one barred their way and they entered the main tunnel. To their right they could see their big ports beyond which stood their ship.

Supplies were scattered along the walls. Space suits hung on pegs. Weapons were racked.

"Come along," said Angel.

They confronted the first series of doors which led to Slavinsky. In the first, second and third chambers they found no one. The fourth was locked.

Angel waved Whittaker back and from the second chamber sighted with the bazooka on the locked door.

"Look alive in case anybody comes," said Angel.

Whittaker placed the missile and then stepped aside, Tommy gun ready.

The trajectory of the rocket flamed out. Smoke and dust

dissolved the far door. The echoing concussion buffeted them, unheard through their suits.

Angel was up with a rush, cleaving the billows of cordite. His charge brought him straight into the inner sanctum.

And there, pistol gripped but flung back, was Slavinsky.

The black eyes glared. The yellow teeth showed. Whatever he yelled Angel could not hear. The pistol jerked and a cartridge empty flipped up.

Angel chopped down with the Tommy gun.

And discovered the engineering fact that metal still fifty degrees below zero centigrade does not work well. The firing pin fell short.

The lucite casque fanned out a gauzy pattern but the slug did not penetrate, leaving only a blot.

Angel threw the gun straight at Slavinsky's head. Slavinsky ducked the weapon. But he did not duck the chair which followed it. He staggered back, losing his grip on the pistol.

In Angel's radio, Whittaker's voice yelled, "Three Ruskies are comin'!"

"Use a grenade!" cried Angel. And he flung himself bodily upon Slavinsky.

The metal mittens were clumsy and could not find the general's throat. Slavinsky got a heel into Angel's belt and catapulted him with a smash against the ceiling.

Angel flung himself back. Slavinsky's naked torso was nothing to grip.

"Get him!" howled Whittaker. "They got us penned in!"

Angel grabbed for the sling of the Tommy gun. The weapon leaped up, amazingly light. But it had mass and mass counted.

He drove the butt through Slavinsky's guard, drove in the teeth, the nose, brought sheets of blood into the eyes, crushed the jutting jaw and obliterated the face.

He spun about to find Whittaker holding a bulging door. Angel reached into his kit and pulled out a flask.

"Let them in!"

"They're in!" roared Whittaker.

The bottle of lewisite exploded against the wall beside the first Russian, spraying out over his naked skin.

The rest plowed forward. They plowed, caught their throats, strangled and dropped.

Angel turned and popped a space cloak and helmet on the remains of Slavinsky. He wanted him alive before the gas reached clear across the chamber. "Stay here," said Angel. And he plunged out.

He found Boyd in a cell, safe enough, carefully garbed in his space helmet.

"It was horrible," said Boyd. "The fools grabbed those cigarettes like you said they would. They distributed all of them to everybody but Slavinsky and he hits marijuana instead. And then they started to light up. Even them that didn't get to take a puff got it from the rest. Lootenant, don't never feed me no lewisite cigarette!"

"Anybody else you know of back here?" said Angel sweetly.

"Whoever survived rushed up to where you came in. Geez, Lootenant, what if that had missed?"

"We'd be working in St. Peter's army," grinned Angel. "Keep that helmet on. This whole place must be full of gas."

They went back to Slavinsky's office and from there made way into the communications center.

Boyd set the wave lengths and called.

When they had Washington as though they were Russians, Angel took the aircraft code from his kit and began to give them news that Russia wouldn't know in time.

"We have met Slavinsky," he coded. "I am in possession of this objective and require reinforcements immediately. The enemy is dead except for stragglers outside who will die. Tell the highest in command to send force quickly. We are victorious!"

Whittaker put an affectionate hand on Angel's shoulder and shook it gently. Angel felt terrible.

"Lieutenant," said the surgeon, "you'd better come around. It's nearly time."

The watch on his wrist gleamed as hugely as a steeple clock and said, "Zero three fifty-one" in an unnecessarily loud voice.

He was dressed somehow and they shoved him into the corridor, which was at least half the distance to Mars. A potted palm fell down and became a general.

"Fine morning, fine morning, Lieutenant. You look fit. Fit, sir. No clouds and a splendid full moon."

The aide was brilliant. Angel knew him well. The aide had been an upperclassman when Angel was at the Point.

"Beg pardon, sir," said the aide sidewise to the general. "But we've just time to brief him as we ride down. Here, this way, Lieutenant."

When they were in the car the aide said, "You have been

thoroughly briefed before. But there must be a quick resumé unless you think you are thoroughly cognizant of your duties."

Angel would have answered but all that came out was a groan.

"You will phone all data back to us. Our tests show that the wave can travel much farther than that. Anything you may think important, beyond maps and perhaps geology, you are permitted to note and report.

"Under no circumstances are you to attempt to change any control settings in your ship. All instructions are in this packet."

Angel shoved the brown packet into his pocket with a twinge of pain. *What* a hangover. And what a dreadfully confused night he had had!

Colonel Anthony got him out of the car, through the crowd and up the ladder.

Whittaker was standing there, indolently chewing tobacco. Metal glinted behind them in the interior. Commander Dawson of the Navy prowled around the ship and then went to take his post.

"You've got a week to sober up, my boy," said Anthony.

"I'll be fine," said Angel, managing a smile.

Angel stepped from the ladder to the platform.

"Board!" shouted Dawson.

Floodlights and cameras and upraised faces. There was a hushed, awed stillness.

Boyd had a big pair of glasses fixed upon the full moon. He was adjusting them to get the proper focus. Suddenly Angel grabbed the glasses away and stabbed them at the brilliant orb.

With a little sigh of relief he gave the glasses back and with a wave of his hand to the crowd, entered the ship.

The door closed. The spectators were waved hurriedly back.

There was a crash of jets, a flash of metal.

The spaceship was gone.

In spite of nightmares and hangovers, Man had begun his first flight into outer space.

Story Preview

NOW that you've just ventured through some of the captivating tales in the Stories from the Golden Age collection by L. Ron Hubbard, turn the page and enjoy a preview of *The Great Secret*. Join Fanner Marston, a man whose greed and lust for power drives him through a blistering desert to the legendary city of Parva, where a secret awaits which will give him absolute control over all the universe.

The Great Secret

SWEEPING clouds shadowed the tawny plain, and far off in the east the plumes of night spread gently, mournfully, burying the corpse of the Livian day. Fanner Marston, a tattered speck upon a ridge, looked eastward, looked to the glory he sought and beheld it.

Throat and tongue swollen with thirst, green eyes blazing now with new ecstasy, he knew he had it. He would gain it, would realize that heady height upon which he had elected to stand. Before him lay the Great Secret! The Secret which had made a dead race rule the Universe! And that Secret would be his, Fanner Marston's, and Fanner Marston would be the ruler, the new ruler, the arbiter of destiny for all the Universe!

All through these weeks he had stumbled over the gutted plains toward these blue mountains beneath the scorching double sun. He had suffered agonies but he had won!

There, glittering in the yellow sunlight was Parva, dead, beautiful city of the ancients, city of the blessed, city of knowledge and power.

Fanner laughed. He was strong; he was lean; but he was not handsome; and of all the things about him this laugh, distorted by thirst-ravaged lips, was the least pleasant. His eyes, which had of late grown so very dull, flamed greenly with the ecstasy which came with that vision.

He had won. They had told him that he could not; the legends said it was not possible for any mortal man to win. But the spell of the ancients was broken, their books were open, their riches lay for the taking. Parva was there! Parva was his!

It mattered nothing to Fanner that nearly twenty miles of gashed and forbidding terrain still lay between him and his goal. It mattered not that his canteens were empty; nor did it matter that, behind the ridge on which he stood, his monocycle, last vehicle of his caravan, was a ruined wreck.

He was glad now that his companions were dead—of thirst, of quarrels, of disease. He would not have to murder the last of them now and so preserve to himself this incalculable thing which awaited him. Fate was shaping everything for him!

He could do these twenty miles by noon of the next day, do them the hard way, on foot and without water, for there was something to sustain him now; he knew that the city was real, had truly existed through all these ages, was just as the history books had said it was. And if this much was true, then all was true. And he had seen the silver river!

Fanner's boots were scuffed relics but he set forth down the rocky slope and so great was his ecstasy that he did not feel the sharp bites of the rocks, nor did he feel the fingers of thirst which were throttling him. He was hard; he could outlive forty men and had done it; he would succeed, for he was Fanner Marston!

He had fought these deserts and mountains and he had whipped them—almost. He would live through to the end, and see the Great Secret which awaited him emblazon his name throughout space!

Fanner Marston would bring a new era, a day when spaceships no longer had to land in seas to save themselves from being shattered, when men would be hampered no longer in combating the atmospheres of many now uninhabitable planets. The wealth of the Universe would be his for the taking; the entire race of mankind would bow to his command like vassals. For there, glittering in the sunset, was Parva—Parva, the city of the Great Secret.

Darkness caught him, and he groped his stumbling way among a great forest of black boulders. He did not mind the shocks of falling, the cuts inflicted upon him, the gouges of the unkind earth; nor did he mind the constantly increasing size of his tongue. Distance he had mastered; mere thirst would not stop him now. And besides, he had seen it, just like in the legends. The silver river. What cared he for thirst when that mighty stream awaited him?

Fanner Marston, master of the Universe: it was a pleasant title to resound through his brain.

Black-mouthed with thirst, stumbling with fatigue, lightheaded with his dream of power, he struggled on through the night.

To find out more about *The Great Secret* and how you can obtain your copy, go to www.goldenagestories.com.

Glossary

STORIES FROM THE GOLDEN AGE *reflect the words and expressions used in the 1930s and 1940s, adding unique flavor and authenticity to the tales. While a character's speech may often reflect regional origins, it also can convey attitudes common in the day. So that readers can better grasp such cultural and historical terms, uncommon words or expressions of the era, the following glossary has been provided.*

arc light: the light produced by a lamp where electric current flows across the gap between two electrodes.

azimuth compass: a compass with azimuth bearings to indicate direction. Azimuth bearings use all 360° of a compass to indicate direction. The compass is numbered clockwise with north as 0° and then, moving clockwise, due east 90°, due south 180° and due west 270°. So a bearing of 45° would be northeast and a bearing of 225° would be southwest, and so on.

barques: sailing ships with three to five masts.

beta rays: streams of particles emitted during radioactive decay.

bilge: worthless talk; nonsense.

blathery: unsubstantial; rotten; trashy.

blue eyed: having or representing childlike innocence.

brass hats: high-ranking officers.

casque: any helmet-shaped head covering.

chaw: a wad of chewing tobacco.

Congressional Medal of Honor: the highest military decoration in the United States, presented by the president in the name of Congress, to members of the armed forces for gallantry and bravery beyond the call of duty in action against an enemy.

cordial: a sweet-flavored alcoholic drink usually considered an after-meal beverage.

cordite: a family of smokeless propellants, developed and produced in the United Kingdom from the late nineteenth century to replace gunpowder as a military propellant for large weapons, such as tank guns, artillery and naval guns. Cordite is now obsolete and no longer produced.

deep-ended: be in a situation where expertise or experience is required.

emplacements: prepared positions for weapons or military equipment.

Eternal, by the: used to express surprise or emphasis; *the Eternal* refers to God.

flimdoodle, don't give a: variation of "don't give a hoot"; to not care about something at all.

full astern: a naval order where the engines are reversed to bring the ship to a stop. Used here to mean "put a stop to."

G-men: government men; agents of the Federal Bureau of Investigation.

gouts: masses.

hackies: cab drivers.

Japanese moon: refers to a time of the year when the moon is said to be the brightest and most beautiful, which is celebrated in Japan.

K and D and C rations: military combat food introduced by the United States Army during World War II. K-ration: a field or combat ration designed for minimal preparation, using canned, precooked or freeze-dried foods, powdered beverage mixes and concentrated food bars. K-rations were intended to be used for only two or three days, but soldiers being forced to consume them for weeks at a time led to the ration's lack of popularity. D-ration: bars of concentrated chocolate combined with other ingredients to provide a high-calorie content (intended as an emergency ration). C-ration: a complete meal in a can, ready to eat, requiring no special preparation or storage.

lampblack: a black pigment made from soot.

lewisite: a colorless or brownish oily poisonous liquid used in gaseous form in chemical warfare.

lucite: a transparent or translucent plastic.

Madrillon: the name of a supper club in Washington, DC, that featured Latin music and jazz.

manifestos: public declarations of policies and aims.

Mussorgsky: reference to the musical scores "Songs and Dances of Death," written by Modest Mussorgsky (1839–1881), a Russian composer of operas and orchestral works. He strove to achieve a uniquely Russian musical identity, often in deliberate defiance of the established conventions of Western music.

Old Dutch cleanser: a white scouring powder used as a sink, stove and tub cleaner in the 1930s.

Ole Mule: chewing tobacco.

rills: narrow straight valleys on the moon's surface.

Scheherazade: the female narrator of *The Arabian Nights*, who during one thousand and one adventurous nights saved her life by entertaining her husband, the king, with stories.

school solution: the authoritatively announced policies and practices of a group, such as the military way of doing things. Used humorously.

SECNAV: Secretary of the Navy.

Smyth report: report written at the end of World War II that told the official story of the making of the atomic bomb. Because it discussed what had been top-secret information, the material it represented was, by definition, no longer classified and could therefore be discussed openly.

sotto voce: in a low, soft voice so as not to be overheard.

sprites: small or delicately built people who are likened to elves or fairies.

stroboscopic: the illusion of a moving or rotating object being stationery.

toils: an entrapment; something that binds, snares or entangles one.

Tommy gun: Thompson submachine gun; a light portable automatic machine gun.

transit: a surveying instrument surmounted by a telescope that can be rotated completely around its horizontal axis, used for measuring vertical and horizontal angles.

Trotskyite: a supporter of Trotskyism, the political and economic theories of Communism as advocated by Leon Trotsky (1879–1940) usually including the principle of worldwide revolution. His politics differed sharply from those of Stalinism and after leading the failed struggle against the policies and rise of Joseph Stalin in the 1920s, Trotsky was expelled from the Communist Party and deported from the Soviet Union. While in exile in Mexico, he was assassinated by a Soviet agent.

Tycho: a prominent crater on the face of the moon about fifty-six miles in diameter.

vassals: servants or slaves.

Waldorf: The Waldorf=Astoria; a famous hotel in New York City known for its high standards and as a social center for the city.

West Point: US Military Academy in New York. It has been a military post since 1778 and the seat of the US Military Academy since 1802.

L. Ron Hubbard
in the Golden Age
of Pulp Fiction

*In writing an adventure story
a writer has to know that he is adventuring
for a lot of people who cannot.
The writer has to take them here and there
about the globe and show them
excitement and love and realism.
As long as that writer is living the part of an
adventurer when he is hammering
the keys, he is succeeding with his story.*

*Adventuring is a state of mind.
If you adventure through life, you have a
good chance to be a success on paper.*

*Adventure doesn't mean globe-trotting,
exactly, and it doesn't mean great deeds.
Adventuring is like art.
You have to live it to make it real.*

—*L. RON HUBBARD*

L. Ron Hubbard
and American
Pulp Fiction

B ORN March 13, 1911, L. Ron Hubbard lived a life at least as expansive as the stories with which he enthralled a hundred million readers through a fifty-year career.

Originally hailing from Tilden, Nebraska, he spent his formative years in a classically rugged Montana, replete with the cowpunchers, lawmen and desperadoes who would later people his Wild West adventures. And lest anyone imagine those adventures were drawn from vicarious experience, he was not only breaking broncs at a tender age, he was also among the few whites ever admitted into Blackfoot society as a bona fide blood brother. While if only to round out an otherwise rough and tumble youth, his mother was that rarity of her time—a thoroughly educated woman—who introduced her son to the classics of Occidental literature even before his seventh birthday.

But as any dedicated L. Ron Hubbard reader will attest, his world extended far beyond Montana. In point of fact, and as the son of a United States naval officer, by the age of eighteen he had traveled over a quarter of a million miles. Included therein were three Pacific crossings to a then still mysterious Asia, where he ran with the likes of Her British Majesty's agent-in-place

L. Ron Hubbard, left, at Congressional Airport, Washington, DC, 1931, with members of George Washington University flying club.

for North China, and the last in the line of Royal Magicians from the court of Kublai Khan. For the record, L. Ron Hubbard was also among the first Westerners to gain admittance to forbidden Tibetan monasteries below Manchuria, and his photographs of China's Great Wall long graced American geography texts.

Upon his return to the United States and a hasty completion of his interrupted high school education, the young Ron Hubbard entered George Washington University. There, as fans of his aerial adventures may have heard, he earned his wings as a pioneering barnstormer at the dawn of American aviation. He also earned a place in free-flight record books for the longest sustained flight above Chicago. Moreover, as a roving reporter for *Sportsman Pilot* (featuring his first professionally penned articles), he further helped inspire a generation of pilots who would take America to world airpower.

Immediately beyond his sophomore year, Ron embarked on the first of his famed ethnological expeditions, initially to then untrammeled Caribbean shores (descriptions of which would later fill a whole series of West Indies mystery-thrillers). That the Puerto Rican interior would also figure into the future of Ron Hubbard stories was likewise no accident. For in addition to cultural studies of the island, a 1932–33

LRH expedition is rightly remembered as conducting the first complete mineralogical survey of a Puerto Rico under United States jurisdiction.

There was many another adventure along this vein: As a lifetime member of the famed Explorers Club, L. Ron Hubbard charted North Pacific waters with the first shipboard radio direction finder, and so pioneered a long-range navigation system universally employed until the late twentieth century. While not to put too fine an edge on it, he also held a rare Master Mariner's license to pilot any vessel, of any tonnage in any ocean.

Yet lest we stray too far afield, there is an LRH note at this juncture in his saga, and it reads in part:

"I started out writing for the pulps, writing the best I knew, writing for every mag on the stands, slanting as well as I could."

To which one might add: His earliest submissions date from the summer of 1934, and included tales drawn from true-to-life Asian adventures, with characters roughly modeled on British/American intelligence operatives he had known in Shanghai. His early Westerns were similarly peppered with details drawn from personal

Capt. L. Ron Hubbard in Ketchikan, Alaska, 1940, on his Alaskan Radio Experimental Expedition, the first of three voyages conducted under the Explorers Club flag.

experience. Although therein lay a first hard lesson from the often cruel world of the pulps. His first Westerns were soundly rejected as lacking the authenticity of a Max Brand yarn (a particularly frustrating comment given L. Ron Hubbard's Westerns came straight from his Montana homeland, while Max Brand was a mediocre New York poet named Frederick Schiller Faust, who turned out implausible six-shooter tales from the terrace of an Italian villa).

Nevertheless, and needless to say, L. Ron Hubbard persevered and soon earned a reputation as among the most publishable names in pulp fiction, with a ninety percent placement rate of first-draft manuscripts. He was also among the most prolific, averaging between seventy and a hundred thousand words a month. Hence the rumors that L. Ron Hubbard had redesigned a typewriter for faster keyboard action and pounded out manuscripts on a continuous roll of butcher paper to save the precious seconds it took to insert a single sheet of paper into manual typewriters of the day.

That all L. Ron Hubbard stories did not run beneath said byline is yet another aspect of pulp fiction lore. That is, as publishers periodically rejected manuscripts from top-drawer authors if only to avoid paying top dollar, L. Ron Hubbard and company just as frequently replied with submissions under various pseudonyms. In Ron's case, the list

A MAN OF MANY NAMES

Between 1934 and 1950, L. Ron Hubbard authored more than fifteen million words of fiction in more than two hundred classic publications. To supply his fans and editors with stories across an array of genres and pulp titles, he adopted fifteen pseudonyms in addition to his already renowned L. Ron Hubbard byline.

Winchester Remington Colt
Lt. Jonathan Daly
Capt. Charles Gordon
Capt. L. Ron Hubbard
Bernard Hubbel
Michael Keith
Rene Lafayette
Legionnaire 148
Legionnaire 14830
Ken Martin
Scott Morgan
Lt. Scott Morgan
Kurt von Rachen
Barry Randolph
Capt. Humbert Reynolds

included: Rene Lafayette, Captain Charles Gordon, Lt. Scott Morgan and the notorious Kurt von Rachen—supposedly on the lam for a murder rap, while hammering out two-fisted prose in Argentina. The point: While L. Ron Hubbard as Ken Martin spun stories of Southeast Asian intrigue, LRH as Barry Randolph authored tales of romance on the Western range—which, stretching between a dozen genres is how he came to stand among the two hundred elite authors providing close to a million tales through the glory days of American Pulp Fiction.

L. Ron Hubbard, circa 1930, at the outset of a literary career that would finally span half a century.

In evidence of exactly that, by 1936 L. Ron Hubbard was literally leading pulp fiction's elite as president of New York's American Fiction Guild. Members included a veritable pulp hall of fame: Lester "Doc Savage" Dent, Walter "The Shadow" Gibson, and the legendary Dashiell Hammett—to cite but a few.

Also in evidence of just where L. Ron Hubbard stood within his first two years on the American pulp circuit: By the spring of 1937, he was ensconced in Hollywood, adopting a Caribbean thriller for Columbia Pictures, remembered today as *The Secret of Treasure Island*. Comprising fifteen thirty-minute episodes, the L. Ron Hubbard screenplay led to the most profitable matinée serial in Hollywood history. In accord with Hollywood culture, he was thereafter continually called

The 1937 Secret of Treasure Island, *a fifteen-episode serial adapted for the screen by L. Ron Hubbard from his novel,* Murder at Pirate Castle.

upon to rewrite/doctor scripts—most famously for long-time friend and fellow adventurer Clark Gable.

In the interim—and herein lies another distinctive chapter of the L. Ron Hubbard story—he continually worked to open Pulp Kingdom gates to up-and-coming authors. Or, for that matter, anyone who wished to write. It was a fairly unconventional stance, as markets were already thin and competition razor sharp. But the fact remains, it was an L. Ron Hubbard hallmark that he vehemently lobbied on behalf of young authors—regularly supplying instructional articles to trade journals, guest-lecturing to short story classes at George Washington University and Harvard, and even founding his own creative writing competition. It was established in 1940, dubbed the Golden Pen, and guaranteed winners both New York representation and publication in *Argosy*.

But it was John W. Campbell Jr.'s *Astounding Science Fiction* that finally proved the most memorable LRH vehicle. While every fan of L. Ron Hubbard's galactic epics undoubtedly knows the story, it nonetheless bears repeating: By late 1938, the pulp publishing magnate of Street & Smith was determined to revamp *Astounding Science Fiction* for broader readership. In particular, senior editorial director F. Orlin Tremaine called for stories with a stronger *human element*. When acting editor John W. Campbell balked, preferring his spaceship-driven tales,

Tremaine enlisted Hubbard. Hubbard, in turn, replied with the genre's first truly *character-driven* works, wherein heroes are pitted not against bug-eyed monsters but the mystery and majesty of deep space itself—and thus was launched the Golden Age of Science Fiction.

The names alone are enough to quicken the pulse of any science fiction aficionado, including LRH friend and protégé, Robert Heinlein, Isaac Asimov, A. E. van Vogt and Ray Bradbury. Moreover, when coupled with LRH stories of fantasy, we further come to what's rightly been described as the foundation of every modern tale of horror: L. Ron Hubbard's immortal *Fear.* It was rightly proclaimed by Stephen King as one of the very few works to genuinely warrant that overworked term "classic"—as in: *"This is a classic tale of creeping, surreal menace and horror. . . . This is one of the really, really good ones."*

To accommodate the greater body of L. Ron Hubbard fantasies, Street & Smith inaugurated *Unknown*—a classic pulp if there ever was one, and wherein readers were soon thrilling to the likes of *Typewriter in the Sky* and *Slaves of Sleep* of which Frederik Pohl would declare: *"There are bits and pieces from Ron's work that became part of the language in ways that very few other writers managed."*

L. Ron Hubbard, 1948, among fellow science fiction luminaries at the World Science Fiction Convention in Toronto.

And, indeed, at J. W. Campbell Jr.'s insistence, Ron was regularly drawing on themes from the Arabian Nights and

121

so introducing readers to a world of genies, jinn, Aladdin and Sinbad—all of which, of course, continue to float through cultural mythology to this day.

At least as influential in terms of post-apocalypse stories was L. Ron Hubbard's 1940 *Final Blackout*. Generally acclaimed as the finest anti-war novel of the decade and among the ten best works of the genre ever authored—here, too, was a tale that would live on in ways few other writers imagined. Hence, the later Robert Heinlein verdict: "Final Blackout *is as perfect a piece of science fiction as has ever been written.*"

Like many another who both lived and wrote American pulp adventure, the war proved a tragic end to Ron's sojourn in the pulps. He served with distinction in four theaters and was highly decorated for commanding corvettes in the North Pacific. He was also grievously wounded in combat, lost many a close friend and colleague and thus resolved to say farewell to pulp fiction and devote himself to what it had supported these many years—namely, his serious research.

Portland, Oregon, 1943; L. Ron Hubbard captain of the US Navy subchaser PC 815.

But in no way was the LRH literary saga at an end, for as he wrote some thirty years later, in 1980:

"Recently there came a period when I had little to do. This was novel in a life so crammed with busy years, and I decided to amuse myself by writing a novel that was pure science fiction."

That work was *Battlefield Earth: A Saga of the Year 3000*. It was an immediate *New York Times* bestseller and, in fact, the first international science fiction blockbuster in decades. It was not, however, L. Ron Hubbard's magnum opus, as that distinction is generally reserved for his next and final work: The 1.2 million word *Mission Earth*.

> **Final Blackout**
> *is as perfect*
> *a piece of*
> *science fiction as*
> *has ever*
> *been written.*
>
> —Robert Heinlein

How he managed those 1.2 million words in just over twelve months is yet another piece of the L. Ron Hubbard legend. But the fact remains, he did indeed author a ten-volume *dekalogy* that lives in publishing history for the fact that each and every volume of the series was also a *New York Times* bestseller.

Moreover, as subsequent generations discovered L. Ron Hubbard through republished works and novelizations of his screenplays, the mere fact of his name on a cover signaled an international bestseller. . . . Until, to date, sales of his works exceed hundreds of millions, and he otherwise remains among the most enduring and widely read authors in literary history. Although as a final word on the tales of L. Ron Hubbard, perhaps it's enough to simply reiterate what editors told readers in the glory days of American Pulp Fiction:

He writes the way he does, brothers, because he's been there, seen it and done it!

THE STORIES FROM THE
GOLDEN AGE

Your ticket to adventure starts here with the Stories from
the Golden Age collection by master storyteller L. Ron Hubbard.
These gripping tales are set in a kaleidoscope of exotic locales and brim
with fascinating characters, including some of the
most vile villains, dangerous dames and brazen heroes
you'll ever get to meet.

The entire collection of over one hundred and fifty stories is being
released in a series of eighty books and audiobooks.
For an up-to-date listing of available titles,
go to www.goldenagestories.com.

AIR ADVENTURE

Arctic Wings	*Man-Killers of the Air*
The Battling Pilot	*On Blazing Wings*
Boomerang Bomber	*Red Death Over China*
The Crate Killer	*Sabotage in the Sky*
The Dive Bomber	*Sky Birds Dare!*
Forbidden Gold	*The Sky-Crasher*
Hurtling Wings	*Trouble on His Wings*
The Lieutenant Takes the Sky	*Wings Over Ethiopia*

FAR-FLUNG ADVENTURE

SEA ADVENTURE

TALES FROM THE ORIENT

The Devil—With Wings *Pearl Pirate*
The Falcon Killer *The Red Dragon*
Five Mex for a Million *Spy Killer*
Golden Hell *Tah*
The Green God *The Trail of the Red Diamonds*
Hurricane's Roar *Wind-Gone-Mad*
Inky Odds *Yellow Loot*
Orders Is Orders

MYSTERY

The Blow Torch Murder *The Grease Spot*
Brass Keys to Murder *Killer Ape*
Calling Squad Cars! *Killer's Law*
The Carnival of Death *The Mad Dog Murder*
The Chee-Chalker *Mouthpiece*
Dead Men Kill *Murder Afloat*
The Death Flyer *The Slickers*
Flame City *They Killed Him Dead*

FANTASY

SCIENCE FICTION

WESTERN